Murder Under A New Moon

A Mona Moon Mystery
Book Eight

Abigail Keam

Worker Bee Press

Published in the USA by

Worker Bee Press
P.O. Box 485
Nicholasville, KY 40340

Books By Abigail Keam

Josiah Reynolds Mysteries
Death By A HoneyBee I
Death By Drowning II
Death By Bridle III
Death By Bourbon IV
Death By Lotto V
Death By Chocolate VI
Death By Haunting VII
Death By Derby VIII
Death By Design IX
Death By Malice X
Death By Drama XI
Death By Stalking XII
Death By Deceit XIII
Death By Magic XIV
Death By Shock XV
Death By Chance XVI

The Mona Moon Mystery Series
Murder Under A Blue Moon I
Murder Under A Blood Moon II
Murder Under A Bad Moon III
Murder Under A Silver Moon IV
Murder Under A Wolf Moon V
Murder Under A Black Moon VI
Murder Under A Full Moon VII
Murder Under A New Moon VIII

Last Chance For Love Romance Series
Last Chance Motel I
Gasping For Air II
The Siren's Call III
Hard Landing IV
The Mermaid's Carol V

1

"**I** must keep my family name," Mona declared.

"You will, miss. Madeline Mona Moon Farley, Duchess of Brynelleth," the English solicitor replied.

Mona tapped a finger on the conference table. "Mr. Dankworth, I don't think you understand. According to my uncle's will, I and my children must keep our last name legally Moon or we lose everything. We will be cast aside."

The chief solicitor looked aghast. "But Miss Moon, you will be a duchess. Your children will be in line to the English throne."

"That is such poppycock. I care nothing about being a duchess, and my children becoming king or queen of Great Britain is about as likely as me living on the moon. What I care about is being in control of Moon Enterprises. Moon Enterprises is worth twenty times that of the Brynelleth estate."

The main solicitor tore off his pince-nez in frustration. A whiff of his cologne drifted across the room. Some of it must have spilled on his waistcoat in which a pocket watch was tucked away. This was not the type of man to wear a Jaeger-LeCoultre Reverso wristwatch or believe in central heating. "Miss Moon, I don't think you understand the gravity of becoming the wife of His Grace, Duke of Brynelleth. By doing what you propose, you will make His Grace the laughing stock of England. You will not even be in the United States to tend to Moon Enterprises. You'll be residing in England."

"Sir, I don't think you understand the gravity of running Moon Enterprises. I have thousands of employees working for me, not to mention thousands of acres of land to manage. Moon Enterprises brings in millions of dollars every year to be dispensed to these workers and invested back into the company. How much does Brynelleth bring in? How many workers does

Brynelleth have? Maybe a hundred at its height, not to mention that Brynelleth is in debt up to its neck. While Moon Enterprises is mining copper and other ores for the industrial might of the United States, Brynelleth is planting turnips."

Mr. Dankworth slammed shut his file and stood up. Motioning to his staff of two, he stormed out of the Moon conference room in Dexter Deatherage's office located in the new Moon office building on Main Street in Lexington, Kentucky.

Dexter shot a glaring look at Mona. "That went well."

"I noticed you didn't run after them to smooth things out."

"I can't stand those upper class English snobs. They make my teeth ache."

Mona laughed. "You must remember we are going against a thousand years of tradition with those chaps. They still refer to us as those rebellious colonists and expect me to curtsey when they enter a room."

"Egads. Do you really want to marry into that life?"

Mona looked serious. "I love Robert. I really

do. We must find a compromise to make this marriage work, but I will not relinquish Moon Enterprises. I know my duty."

"Robert also has a duty, Mona. Brynelleth is the center of the economy for Robert's part of the world. He can't let his people down either."

Mona threw her hands up. "I know. I know. A lot of people are counting on the two of us." Mona stood up and went to the window, looking out at the bustling street. "I love Robert, but I can live without him, though my life will be dull and dreary. With Robert, my life is filled with joy. I want my life filled with joy, Dexter. Please find a way to make this marriage work."

Dexter took out his pipe and tobacco pouch. "Here is what I recommend. You keep your family moniker as your legal name. In return, you throw money at Brynelleth to bring it up to twentieth century standards such as modern plumbing and electricity."

"Oh, Dexter, you're teasing now. I'm sure Brynelleth has indoor bathrooms and electricity."

"Are you sure? In either case, the roof will be shot. Roofs on all those old estate houses are always in need of replacing. That alone will cost thousands."

"I knew that Brynelleth was in serious debt, but I thought Robert handled that when he went over to visit his father."

"Robert got the debt under control, but he still owes the bank a considerable note."

Mona's brow furrowed. "How much money are we talking about to pay off the debt and refurbish the estate?"

Dexter wrote a figure on a piece of paper and handed it to Mona.

She looked at it and whistled. "That much, eh? Goodness. That's a lot of bananas."

"We can take the money out of the workers' pension fund."

"No. This is a personal matter. Moon Enterprises money is not going to pay a dime for Robert's ancestral home. I will have to shell out from my personal accounts."

"It will leave you broke, Mona."

"Doesn't Bynelleth bring in any income?"

"Pittance."

Mona said, "Okay. Let's throw some money at this and make Robert's lawyers more apt to compromise. For the next ten years, we will give thirty-five percent of my income after taxes and expenses to pay for repairs and upkeep on Brynelleth, but Brynelleth has to make changes. They can't keep doing things like they have done since the 1700s. They must embrace modern farming and housekeeping techniques. Robert will be thrilled at the chance to bring the estate up to new standards. I know that he has been trying to get his leasees to change their farming methods."

"I'll have our new legal eagles take Robert's henchmen around and show them the sights. Ply them with burgoo and bourbon. Maybe then they will listen to reason."

Mona grinned. "Keep them away from the brothels."

"Shame on you for even knowing that houses of ill repute exist in our quaint little hamlet."

Mona was tired of talking about Brynelleth. She pulled back a wisp of her platinum hair. "How is Wilhelmina?"

"Doing better. Much better."

"I feel as though I have neglected her. I've been so busy." Mona thought back to her visit to Washington D.C. and her lunch with Eleanor Roosevelt, which led to deadly spy intrigue. "Why don't we invite Robert's blood hounds plus you and Wilhelmina for brunch on Sunday? Show them real Southern hospitality. Might defrost them a bit."

"Worth a try."

"Maybe I can get Wilhelmina alone to myself for a minute or two."

"She would like that. Thanks."

"Eleven sound okay?"

"We'll be there bright-eyed and bushy-tailed."

Mona gathered her gloves and handbag. "See you on Sunday, Dexter."

"Let me escort you out. I want to show you our new typewriters."

"A pleasure."

Mona and Dexter walked through his executive secretarial office and reception room into the major secretarial pool where six typists were busy. Off to the side of the room were more offices. Dexter had hired two young attorneys—one an expert in business law and the other lawyer worked on mining patents/claims.

Dexter introduced Mona to each worker. She was impressed with the typists' skills and looked over some of their work—most of it letters to various employees and buyers of copper ore. Smiling, Mona shook their hands and welcomed them to Moon Enterprises. Then Dexter took her to the switchboard room where three telephone operators worked. Everything was state of the art and impressive.

Moon Enterprises occupied the top floor of Mona's building with a guard and another receptionist stationed at the elevator. Dexter walked Mona to the lift.

"You don't have to walk me to my car, Dexter. I'll be fine. Besides, I want to pop into the bank," Mona said, pulling on her white gloves.

"Very well. See you on Sunday."

The guard pushed the elevator's button. The door opened to a uniformed operator whose gleaming brass buttons on his maroon jacket matched the highly polished walls of the compartment.

Mona thanked the guard and entered. "First floor, please."

"Yes, ma'am, Miss Moon," he said.

Mona exited on the ground floor and entered the bank she had created to cater to the female patrons. The bank was slowly building up a clientele since many women were working outside the home, and the bank was gaining a reputation for fairness, especially when granting loans at a lower interest rate. More and more farmers sought the Moon Bank's help after so many banks closed their doors in 1933.

Mona conferred briefly with the bank manager and took a copy of the bank's most recent quarterly report, which she stuck in her satchel. Saying goodbye to the bank staff, Mona walked outside to her car. At that moment, Mona spied a chauffeured black Pierce-Arrow sedan with a veiled woman sitting in the back. Mona, along with everyone else, stared as the car drove out of sight.

Mona had just caught a glimpse of Belle Brezing, the most infamous madam in the South.

2

Dotty, Mona's personal secretary, stood at the door of Moon Manor and welcomed Mona home. Taking Mona's gloves and red Robin Hood Tyrolean hat, she asked, "How did it go?"

"Don't ask."

"That bad, huh?"

"They stormed out," Mona whispered.

Dotty grinned. "Don't you just love those stuffed shirts?"

"Speaking of the English, is Lord Bob here?" That was Mona's nickname for Robert Farley, now Duke of Brynelleth. Only Mona called him that, but everyone else still referred to him as Lord Farley even though Robert was now a duke. Tradition and custom was hard to change in the Bluegrass, the gem of Kentucky.

"Yeah. He's waiting for you by the pool, soaking up some sun," Dotty said, giving Mona's calendar a quick glance. One of her tasks was to keep Mona's schedule flowing and to make sure Mona was where she was supposed to be. It showed that Mona was free for the afternoon.

"I think I will join him. Can you have some sandwiches and tea sent out to the garden while I change? I'm starving."

"Sure thing."

"Thank you, Dotty."

"Before you go upstairs, your Aunt Melanie called. She seemed awfully angry about something. Said for you to call her back as soon as possible."

"She's been pestering me for more money."

"I think the underlining cause is your negotiations for marriage to His Grace. Didn't she have her caps set on him before you came along?"

"I'm sure that's why she is so agitated. Melanie will do anything she can to throw a monkey wrench between Robert and me. She can't stand others being happy." Mona sighed, feeling besieged. Would her relatives, especially Aunt Melanie, never give her a moment's peace? "I'll deal with her later. I want to see Robert now. Can you call Melanie back and relate that I'll talk to her next week? I want to get these Brits off my back first."

"I'll call her right now."

"Thank you." Mona checked her platinum hair in the hall mirror next to the coat rack and umbrella stand. She ignored the fact that her galoshes were missing. The house butler, Thomas, disliked having a coat rack and umbrella stand next to the front door. He thought it looked tacky, but Mona liked the convenience. There was a constant battle between the two about it and now Mona's boots were missing. She would have to hunt for them and put them by the front door again.

All Mona's employees quaked at the sight of her, except Moon Manor's household staff, who pretty much did as they pleased. They were determined to make Moon Manor the showplace of the South, and Mona knew the staff expected her to play the part of a great lady. She tried to live up to their expectations, but at times it was all too much. Mona doubted she could live under the more confining restraints of being a duchess.

"Oh, just a minute Dotty." Mona pulled out the bank quarterly report from her satchel. "Can you look over this tomorrow and see where the holes are?"

Dotty took the report and glanced at it. "Looks awfully thin. Do you have the list of depositors?"

Mona winced. "Golly, I forgot to ask for one."

"No never mind. I'll pick up the list on Monday." Dotty gave a beautiful smile. "Because this evening I have a date."

"You cheeky vixen. Who with?"

"The new assistant for Gentry Farms. We're going to see the new Jean Harlow picture."

Mona kept a smile on her face, but she didn't like the fact that Dotty was seeing an employee of Jacob Gentry, who was a vocal provocateur against her. He didn't like women to play a part in public life and used religion to advance his opinions. Mona didn't like Gentry personally or his loudmouth opinions on women. She thought him to be a filthy man, both spiritually and physically. More than one person had come to warn Mona of the disturbing things Gentry was saying about her.

"Where did you meet this young man?"

"At a mixer for professionals at the Main Street Baptist Church."

"Baptist churches have mixers?"

"Well, you know, punch and cookies. Just a way for people to meet each other."

"Next you'll be telling me that the Main Street Baptist Church is hosting a cotillion."

Both women laughed as that particular church preached against dancing.

"I've got to change. I hope you have a good time," Mona said.

"Thanks."

Mona started up the stairs and then stopped. "Dotty."

"Yes?"

"I know you realize that you need to be discreet with this young man. Nothing about me or Lord Bob."

For a second, Mona saw a shadow of hurt across Dotty's face. "Of course, Mona. I'll get that order for a lunch tray in for you now. Excuse me, please."

Mona pressed her lips together. She had offended Dotty, but Mona had been betrayed by her previous secretary. Mona did not intend to make the same mistake again. She was determined to keep an eye on Dotty and her new "beau."

At that moment, she heard fussing coming from the kitchen. The head butler, Thomas, and the chef, Monsieur Bisaillon, must be butting heads again. Mona leaned over the banister to listen before heading to her room. Somehow, the arguing was comforting. It was normal. Yes, that's what it was. Normal to hear pots banging, servants moving about, and Thomas arguing with Bisaillon.

It was what Mona wanted—to live a normal life.

She doubted she was going to get it.

3

Mona tiptoed behind and playfully clasped the eyes of Lawrence Robert Emerton Dagobert Farley, now Duke of Brynelleth, as he napped in a lounge chair alongside Chloe, her poodle.

Robert caught her hands and kissed the inside of her palms. "You even taste delicious."

Mona swung around the chair and strutted back and forth. "How do you like my new bathing suit?"

"Va-va-va-voom!" Robert sat up and howled, which caused Chloe to jump off the chair and look about in confusion.

"I guess it meets with your approval."

"I'd like it better if you were wearing nothing at all."

Both Mona and Robert heard the clearing of a

throat. They turned to see Thomas, standing nearby with a tray of sandwiches and a large pitcher of sweet iced tea. Keeping a neutral expression, Thomas asked, "Shall I put the tray on the table, Miss Mona?"

Embarrassed, Mona said, "Yes, thank you, Thomas. That will be all. I'll call if I need you."

"Very good, Miss."

As soon as Thomas was out of sight, Robert burst into laughter. "Mona, you should see your face. You're as red as a beet."

"It's not funny. We never have any privacy. There is always someone lurking about."

"Get used to it, pet. We are basically public people."

"I don't know if I want to get used to it."

Robert asked sharply, "What does that mean?"

Mona wrung her hands. "I don't know. I don't know how to explain it, but I never have any time to myself. Everywhere I go, there are people with expectations and guards following me about. I'm beginning to resent it."

"I take it today didn't go well with the solicitors," Robert said, picking up a roast beef sandwich.

"Robert, I loathe your lawyers."

"They are not my lawyers, darling. They are Brynelleth's men. They don't work for me, but the estate."

"But Robert, you are the estate, aren't you? Can't you tell them to compromise? They were so recalcitrant today."

Robert put down his sandwich, stood and put his arms around Mona, squeezing tight. "Tell me all about it. What happened today?"

Mona leaned into Robert's chest, deeply inhaling his scent of horses, tobacco, and musk. "I feel so . . . I don't know even how I feel. I'm just tired. Exhausted." Despairingly, she thrust her head in her hands. "It's all too much at times."

"Mona! Mona! Dearest. What's the matter? Tell me." Robert sat down in a metal lawn chair and pulled Mona on his lap, cradling her like a small child.

"I don't know what's the matter with me, Robert. I feel ashamed to break down so."

"I know what's the matter. You've worked nonstop for almost two years without a break. That's on top of betrayal, kidnapping, suicide, and murder. That would be enough to send anyone to the booby hatch," Robert teased.

Mona broke into laughter which quickly dissolved into tears.

"Aww, Mona," Robert said, pulling her closer. "I didn't mean to make you weep. It was meant to be a joke."

"I know, but it's not funny."

"You keep everything bottled up inside. I say cut loose and have a good cry. Get it all out of your system. Go on, cry to your heart's content," Robert whispered into her ear. "I won't tell a soul that you're not superhuman."

Mona wrapped her arms around Robert's neck and wept until she began hiccuping. Once the hiccups stopped, Robert made Mona eat a turkey sandwich and take a swim in the heated pool. Afterward, Robert wrapped Mona in a warm, fluffy bathrobe. "Is the crying jag over?"

Mona nodded, nibbling on another sandwich. "I've been holding those tears in for a long time. It was good to get them out. You know, you can cry anytime with me as well."

"I didn't cry when my father died. Not a single tear. I don't think I liked the man. I know I didn't love him. He was so stern and stubborn.

But when my brother and mother died, I cried. I think my brother's death hit me the hardest."

"I know what you mean."

"You need a vacation, Mona."

"I do need some downtime. I think you're right."

"When can we get away?"

"We can't. Your solicitors are breathing down my neck, making demands. Essentially they are asking me to relinquish control of Moon Enterprises, the largest copper mining company in the United States, so I can host dinner parties for you at Brynelleth."

Robert asked, "Would that be so bad?"

"I've made my mark in the world. I'm not going to give it up for marriage."

If Robert was disappointed with Mona's reply, he didn't show it. "It's too bad we can't run off to Italy and live in a palazzo on a mountain top. I'll grow a beard and we'll make money selling our own wine. You can sketch for the tourists in the market place."

"Have you seen my artistic ability? I can barely draw stick people. We'd starve."

"I guess that is that. We'll have to stick with

the current plan." Robert dried off with a towel. "What *is* the current plan?"

"Your people are coming to brunch on Sunday, along with Dexter and Willie. You are to be gallant, but firm in telling them that they have to compromise. I am not going to live in England full time, I will carry the Moon name, and I will still be the head of Moon Enterprises."

"What about being a wife?"

"What about being a partner in life? The term *wife* means subservience to me. I have never liked that marriage phrase—man and wife."

"Mona, we need to be realistic about this. I can't stay in the United States for long periods of time. I need to be at Brynelleth. Things are different now that Father is dead. I have responsibilities."

"You can hire a manager."

"So can you."

"I need to be here as well, Robert. Moon Manor is my home."

"Brynelleth will become your home."

"I told you how I felt even before you proposed. You should never have pursued me if you just wanted a hostess for Brynelleth. I will not budge on this matter."

Robert looked sorrowful as though he had come to some uncomfortable realization. "I guess I better make the lads understand on Sunday."

Mona clasped Robert, "Please, Robert, understand. I can't just be your wife. I must be me as well—Mona Moon, head of Moon Enterprises. Don't ask me to make a choice."

"You would choose Moon Enterprises over me?"

"See how this is turning out? No one is asking you to choose between being a duke and marrying. It's always the woman who has to sacrifice, and I won't do it. If we can't compromise, I will give back your ring."

"Mona, I know you love me. I'll see if I can remove that burr from under your saddle on Sunday."

Mona pushed Robert. "I'm not the one with a problem. You make your men understand that they must come around—not me!"

Robert laughed and swept Mona up in his arms. "Okay. Okay. You don't need to resort to violence."

"If I were going to be violent, I'd crack a vase over your head."

"Which you will probably do one day after we're married. I pity us with our foul tempers."

"Put me down, Robert. The servants will see."

"I've got a better idea, old girl. No one is at my house. Let's play hooky and enjoy ourselves."

"No four course dinner tonight?" Mona's servants, especially Monsieur Bisaillon, insisted Mona dine formally, which included Mona dressing to the nines. Mona considered dinner time a huge time suck and hated its formality.

"How about I fry some good old American hamburgers on the grill?"

"Sounds divine, but Monsieur Bisaillon has been hard at work for tonight's dinner."

"Blast him. Let's do what we want for a change. Were you not just giving me heck about being your own woman and now you cower to your chef's demands? Please, Mona, make up your mind. You're getting heavy."

"Hamburgers sound divine, Lord Bob. Whisk me away."

Delighted, Robert carried Mona through her garden and over to his house, which was next door. Mona clung to his neck, laying her head on his shoulder.

Little did they know the servants were watching from the upstairs windows. They looked at each other and grinned.

Miss Mona would not be coming home tonight.

4

Mona, dressed in a white, gauzy frock with white and black open-toed shoes, fluttered nervously around the luncheon table in the garden. Her only jewelry was a gold locket Robert had given her with the inscription *Forever.* Inside was a picture of Robert and one of them together. Her engagement ring was locked away in her makeup case. She would not wear the engagement ring until they could formally announce it.

"It looks all right to you, Miss Mona?" Thomas asked, putting the last touches on the dinnerware.

"It is perfect," Mona answered, admiring the linen napkins, bone china, and crystal goblets on the garden table found in one of the barns. "Thank you, Mr. Thomas."

Noticing Mona was on edge, Thomas offered, "Miss Mona, it's not my place, but things will work out to your advantage."

"There's an awful lot riding on this brunch," Mona confided. "My future."

"That's not true. Only your choice of this man for your husband is at stake." Thomas shrugged. "If it doesn't work out, maybe Robert Farley wasn't for you. As for your future, you will take care of it just fine."

"Thank you for the vote of confidence."

"Keep your chin up, Miss Mona. We're all rootin' for ya."

Mona smiled. She adored Mr. Thomas. He had been such a help to her since she arrived at Moon Manor. It saddened Mona that he was going to retire soon. Mr. Thomas would be badly missed, although he was training Samuel, who was a splendid fellow.

"MONA!"

Mona looked up and spied Wilhelmina Deatherage crossing the recently-clipped lawn toward her.

"Willie!" Mona cried as she ran toward her friend. They embraced and Mona crooked an arm around her as they made their way to a small sitting area in the garden.

"It's been too long," Willie said, smiling broadly. "You must tell me everything. I hear you had an exciting adventure, but Dexter won't spill." She rolled her eyes at her husband trailing behind.

Mona, noticing the man's perspiring forehead, asked, "Dexter, how are you this morning? You look warm. How about a lemonade?"

"That would be fine," Dexter said, slumping in a chair. "It's warm so early." He tugged at his collar.

"Mr. Thomas, can you bring us some lemonade and iced tea, please?"

"Yes, miss. Coming right up."

"And put ice in the pitchers please. We do have ice, don't we?"

"Yes, miss. We always have blocks of ice since you bought us the extra icebox."

Willie cut in. "Mona, you must tell me about lunch with Eleanor Roosevelt. Did Alice Roosevelt behave at lunch? I hear that she and Eleanor don't get along."

Mona laughed. "Alice did not behave, which

was fun, and the luncheon menu was rather—how should I say this—sparse."

"What does that mean?" Willie asked.

"You know the recipes that Mrs. Roosevelt posts in the papers to help women economize during these dark times. They are created by her cook, Henrietta Nesbitt, who creates meals for five and ten cents per person."

Willie said, "One can't create a meal for two people on twenty cents."

"You can if it is baloney and crackers," Dexter said.

"You can't live on baloney," Willie countered.

"Lots of people are, dear. Many people consider themselves lucky to get it. Besides, I like baloney."

"Every meal?" Willie asked, making a face at her husband. She turned to Mona. "I guess you're telling me lunch was awful."

"Not awful. Just a rather spartan affair. That's all I have to say about it. Mrs. Roosevelt, though, was delightful, very well informed, and I think, a great help to her husband. Violet and I got to spend less than an hour with her, but Mrs. Roosevelt was impressive. I feel the country is in good hands with those two."

"I don't like some of Roosevelt's policies," Dexter said.

"Of course, dear, that's because you're rich," Willie said.

"Thank you, dear. I didn't realize that I was."

Willie said, "You are compared to the rest of the country."

Mona interjected, "Hey, you two, Lord Bob's lawyers will be here soon. Let's demonstrate a united front."

"Quite right," Dexter said. "Willie, behave."

Willie harrumphed, but rallied when Thomas and Samuel brought out trays of lemonade and iced tea. The lemonade had real slices of lemon and maraschino cherries showing through the clear pitchers. "Oh, gracious, real cherries."

Mona felt embarrassed. Only the well-to-do could afford maraschino cherries, but said nothing as she knew the staff were trying their best to impress Robert's solicitors. The cherries were a status symbol. She would speak to Monsieur Bisaillon later about their grocery inventory, although he would balk at any suggestion for economizing. He was her most difficult employee. Mona put those thoughts from her mind, as Robert Farley appeared wearing a dapper navy, pinstriped double-breasted suit.

Dexter rose and shook hands with him. "Good to see you, old man."

Robert bent over and kissed Willie on the cheek. "You look like a girl of sixteen in that frock."

Delighted that someone noticed her new chiffon, flowered print dress, Willie giggled and said, "Get on with your bad self." She patted down her flouncy lapels. "This material is cool, you know."

Robert went over to Mona and gave her a perfunctory peck on the lips. "Are we ready?"

"As much as we ever will be, I guess. Now you will be firm, won't you, Robert?"

"Count on me. I'll be like Nelson raging against Napoleon."

"Oh, goodness no. Nelson died fighting Napoleon," Dexter said, his eyebrows raised in alarm.

Robert suggested, "How about Alexander fighting Darius then?"

"Better."

"Yes, I wouldn't want to be known as a Lady

Hamilton," Mona said, referring to Lady Hamilton's infamous affair with Lord Nelson.

Robert said, "I see I've hit a sour note. I'll just sit down and keep my mouth shut until the solicitors get here."

"That would be advisable, Lord Bob," Mona said, miffed that Robert would make such a comparison. Realizing she was being silly, Mona tried to calm down. The entire luncheon was making her nervous.

Willie patted Mona's hand. "I see everyone is edgy. Let's all have something cool to drink. I'll pour."

"Right you are," Dexter concurred, reaching for a glass of lemonade.

Willie poured lemonade for herself and Dexter and poured two more glasses of iced tea for Mona and Robert. "Wait a minute. Let me put some ice in those glasses." She sighed with pleasure as she used sterling tongs bearing the Moon family crest to place ice from a bucket into the tall glasses. "What a joy it is to have ice during the summer. We are getting a new electric refrigerator this fall, but I'm going to keep my old icebox."

"I don't see why," Dexter remarked. "The refrigerator will keep things cold including drinks."

Robert laughed. "The American obsession with ice."

"Personally, I don't see how Europeans can drink liquids at room temperature, especially beer," Dexter said.

"Dexter likes his beer ice cold," Willie added.

"That I do, indeed, when I have one, which is rare."

Mona shot a look at Willie, who was struggling with alcohol.

"Don't look so worried, Mona. I'm doing fine. Just fine. No need to tiptoe around me about liquor."

Robert, who had his own struggles with alcohol, said, "It gets better with time, Willie."

"Thank you, Robert. It's nice to hear the encouragement."

Dexter stood. "I think I heard a car."

"I do, too," Mona said. She gave Robert a pleading look. "Here we go." She grabbed Robert's hand and gave it a squeeze.

He beamed back at her, before saying, "Sit

down, Dexter. Don't stand up when they are brought out. A duke and his fiancée do not stand for solicitors, and neither shall you."

Dexter promptly sat down and waited, along with the others.

A few minutes later, to everyone's astonishment, Mr. Thomas led Sheriff Monahan out to the garden.

Chagrined, Mona asked, "Sheriff Monahan. I am surprised to see you."

The sheriff tipped his Stetson. "I'm sorry to bust up your party, but I understand three British lawyers were to join you for lunch today."

Robert said, "Yes, we're waiting on them now."

"I'm afraid they won't be coming."

Mona asked, "Why is that?"

"Because two of them are locked up in my jail, and the third one is dead."

5

"WHAT!" exclaimed Mona. "How did this happen?"

Robert jumped to his feet. "Explain, sir."

The sheriff shuffled and looked up rather red-faced. "I'd rather not say in front of the ladies."

Mona said, "Sheriff, you are among adults. Please go on and tell us the news."

The sheriff cast a glance at Mr. Thomas.

Mr. Thomas, who recognized he was not needed, discreetly left. He, too, wanted to learn about the English gentlemen, but knew Mona would tell him later.

Looking about to see if anyone else was listening, Sheriff Monahan said, "It would seem the three gentlemen visited a bawdy house, got drunk, passed out, but the youngest became acquainted with one of the ladies and was found dead in her bed this morning."

"Did he die with a smile on his lips?" Dexter quipped.

"No, sir, he died with an ice pick in his chest. It was murder!"

6

Mona's jaw dropped. She was shocked that the three prestigious and very conservative Brynelleth lawyers would visit such an establishment. "How did it happen?"

"We're not sure, Miss Mona. We're still investigating, but I wanted to tell you first before the newspapers got wind of it. You've got a nasty mess on your hands."

"How may we help, Sheriff?" Robert asked.

"Well, I'd like to ask you a few questions."

Dexter and Willie rose. "We'll leave you be."

"I would like to talk with you, too, Mr. Deatherage. I have some questions for you as well."

"We'll be waiting in the house, sir. Come, Willie. Let's give them some privacy." Dexter escorted Willie to the library in Moon Manor.

Robert pulled out a chair for the sheriff.

"May I pour you an iced tea or lemonade, Sheriff?" Mona asked.

"I'm mighty partial to lemonade, miss."

Mona poured the lemonade and handed it to him. Mona made sure plenty of ice was in his glass, as she waited patiently for him to speak.

Taking off his Stetson, Sheriff Monahan wiped his shiny forehead before replacing it. His shirt showed signs of sweat down its back.

"May I get you something to eat?"

"No, miss. This is unpleasant, but I've got to ask—Lord Farley, where were you last night?"

Farley was about to correct the usage of the title of *lord*, now that he was a duke, but decided it would be petty to correct the man. "I was here from three in the afternoon until about dinner time."

"Where were you after that?"

"I was at home."

"Can anyone corroborate that, sir?"

"No, I was alone."

Mona interrupted, "Sheriff, Robert Farley is trying to protect my reputation. I was with him all night at his house."

"All night?"

Mona cocked her head. "Yes, all night."

The sheriff shot a look at Robert, who grinned somewhat nonplussed.

Robert said, "We are over twenty-one and engaged to be married."

"I see. Did not know."

Robert said, "I would appreciate if it was kept quiet. I'm sure you understand."

"Of course." The sheriff shifted in his seat uncomfortably. "The two men say they work for you, Lord Farley."

"They work for the Brynelleth estate, my ancestral home. Now that my father has died, I am a duke, and since my bride-to-be is an American, some details need to be worked out."

"You need three lawyers to do that?"

"That's what I say," Mona added, curling her lip.

Robert made a face at Mona.

Monahan asked, "How do I address you now that you are a duke?"

"Your Grace."

The sheriff smiled sarcastically. "I guess when

you are in the States, folks will just refer to you as Lord Farley. I don't think we'll go for this *your grace* hooey. It was hard enough to shove *Lord Farley* down our throats."

Insulted, Robert hid his anger and said, "As you wish."

"Now why were these men coming here to-day?"

"It has to do with my future children's inheritance of Brynelleth. The estate has been in my family for many generations. I want to make sure it stays in my family for many generations more."

"I don't follow. If you and Miss Mona have children, won't they inherit the estate?"

"Only the oldest male."

Sheriff Monahan looked surprised.

Mona added, "You see, Sheriff Monahan, England practices primogeniture—an outdated form of feudal inheritance where the oldest male takes all. The rest of the children are left with nothing."

"It's done to keep the estate intact in the family," Robert defended.

"So these men were over here to argue this fact because Miss Mona was putting up a stink?"

One could tell the sheriff enjoyed the revelation.

"There is some disagreement. Miss Moon does not understand our customs."

Mona said, "I understand them all right. Just don't agree with them."

"Darling, please. The sheriff is not interested in our petty squabbles."

"Actually, I am. Do you think these legal disputes could have anything to do with this lawyer's death?"

"I don't see how," answered Robert.

"Perhaps a loyal servant of yours or Miss Moon's was angry enough to do the man in?"

Robert replied, "We don't discuss our personal affairs with the servants."

"Yes, but employees hear things. Miss Mona, you must have loyal servants."

Mona reared back. "No one who will kill for me, Sheriff. You are barking up the wrong tree."

"Do any of your people know of this dilemma?"

"Dexter Deatherage, of course."

"His wife?"

"Yes."

"Anyone else?"

"My secretary, Dotty, and Violet, my maid. Surely, you are not going to accuse these women of sneaking into a bordello and shoving an ice pick into a man's chest? It's ridiculous even to suggest. They have never even laid eyes on these men. The lawyers were to come here today. We were hoping to hammer out a verbal agreement."

Robert asked, "What about the woman the man was with?"

"She has an alibi. Apparently, after they were finished, he fell asleep, and she went downstairs to play cards. Five other people attest to this."

Robert suggested, "She could have killed him before she came downstairs."

"We don't think so. The body was still warm when my men got there. The others said she came downstairs around one this morning. She went back upstairs around seven and discovered the body."

"Maybe the witnesses are lying, Sheriff?"

"Crossed my mind, but I had the word of the madam. She wouldn't lie."

"Whose house of ill-repute was this?" Mona asked.

"Belle Brezing's place, Miss Mona. It was at Belle's."

7

Belle Brezing was a notorious madam, who was the proprietor of the most famous whorehouse in the South.

"It was my understanding that Mrs. Brezing was retired," Mona said, thunderstruck, having had a glimpse of Belle Brezing only yesterday.

"She is for the most part, Miss Mona, but it is my understanding that she keeps a couple of girls for special guests. The brothel is closed to the general public."

"How did my men even know about Belle Brezing?" Robert asked. "Did they say?"

"Apparently through Dexter Deatherage."

Mona bristled. "I don't believe it. Dexter would never have shown them to a house of questionable virtue. Never. He's a boy scout if there ever was one."

Sheriff Monahan said, "I intend to ask him."

"Yes, I would like to know," Robert said, jumping out of his seat.

It gave the sheriff a start.

Robert asked, "What are the other two solicitors charged with?"

"Nothing at the moment. They are in the drunk tank. We'll let them loose after they sober up and answer a few questions. One thing though."

"What's that?"

"They are not to leave town until I get this murder straightened out."

"They will abide by your orders, Sheriff. I'll make sure of it."

Robert held out his hand to shake the sheriff's.

Mona walked the sheriff into the library for his talk with the Deatherages, and then went into the kitchen to tell Monsieur Bisaillon about three less for lunch. She was astonished to find Mr. Thomas, Samuel, Obadiah, and Jedediah gossiping with the irritated French chef, who was lamenting over his unserved lunch. They all went mute when they saw Mona enter the kitchen.

She noticed the windows and doors to the kitchen were open. "I suppose you all heard."

The servants abruptly scattered except for Mr. Thomas and Monsieur Bisaillon, who clucked disapprovingly at Mona.

Mr. Thomas stepped forward. "This is only a minor setback, child. Hold your head up high."

Mona said, "Thank you for your support, Mr. Thomas. Please give instructions to the staff that they are not to discuss this murder or my impending marriage with Robert Farley to anyone. And I mean anyone. It will be cause for immediate dismissal."

"Yes, miss."

"And Monsieur Bisaillon."

The chef's eyes widened as he pressed his lips together before speaking, "Yes, miss?"

"Close the kitchen doors and windows. You are letting the flies in."

Looking sheepish, the chef said, "Yes, Miss Mona."

"I will let you know when I want lunch served."

"Yes, miss."

Feeling in control again, Mona strode back out to the garden, not knowing what to say to Robert. She didn't believe in omens, but this was a sad prelude to her marriage to Robert.

A very sad prelude, indeed.

8

Lunch was a solemn affair. Mona picked at her food while Willie attempted to tell jokes she had heard on the radio.

Trying to break the tension, Willie asked, "Did you hear the Jack Benny show the other night? He had on Bing Crosby. I just love Jack Benny. He's so funny. I wish I could see him for real instead of hearing him on the radio." She turned to Dexter. "Do you think you could take me to New York to see the Jack Benny show? I would really enjoy that, Dexter."

Dexter lifted his head. "What, dear? What did you say?"

Frustrated, Willie threw down her napkin. "Now listen, folks. We've been in tougher spots than this. Let's not be so down in the mouth about it."

Mona blinked several times. "I don't know, Willie. This involves another country now and Robert's future as duke. Once this hits the papers, Moon Enterprises will be adversely affected."

"Silly nonsense, Mona. No one is going to cancel their copper orders because of this," Willie said.

"Aunt Melanie will ask the board to vote me off as head of Moon Enterprises."

"Can she do that?"

"Not really, but she will make lots of trouble for me with our investors. Erode confidence in me."

"The best thing for you to do is to have a party."

"Oh, Willie, don't be daft. This is no time for a party."

"It's the best time for a party. You will see who supports you by who accepts the invitation. Invite some of your fancy friends like Alice Roosevelt. She can invite her fancy society friend, Mona Williams. Once a person like her accepts, others will follow. The gossip will die down. Your Aunt Melanie will not have a leg to stand on. In fact, make it your engagement party."

Robert looked questioningly at Mona. "Well, old girl. Want to give it a twirl?"

"Let me think on it. I need to know where we stand at the moment. Dexter, what happened?"

"After Sheriff Monahan left, I made some calls. The entire Moon office staff is coming in at three this afternoon. I also took the liberty of having two of the Pinkerton boys pick up the Brits. Since there was no charge, their being in jail will not be listed in the public record. I have ensconced them on Robert's farm in a worker's home. They have no phone and no car. That should keep them quiet for a while, at least."

"I have a mind to send them home," Robert said, angrily. "What, in the blazes, induced them to go to a whorehouse? It seems so out-of-character for them."

Dexter said, "We'll find out, but in the meantime, they have to stay until this mess is cleared up. Look on the bright side, though. Mona, you can demand anything you want. The Brynelleth bunch wouldn't dare oppose you now."

Mona instructed Dexter, "Write up a pre-marriage proposal and if Robert agrees to it, I'll sign. I'm tired of my life being put on hold because of old men and their out-dated conceptions. The long-standing way of doing things is strangling our society and holding women back. I want to help put a stop to that."

"All by yourself, darling?" Robert asked, mischievously. "That's a pretty tall order."

"I used the word *help*."

"Now that is settled, let's enjoy our lunch," Willie encouraged. She dove into her salmon mousse. "Delicious."

"Yes, Monsieur Bisaillon put on the dog. He's sulking in the kitchen right now because the lawyers are absent. He's complaining about 'all that work for nothing!'"

Dexter asked, "How do you stand his tantrums? I would have fired him months ago."

Mona replied, "You're tasting the reason why. Besides, Mr. Thomas keeps him in line."

"Can we get back to the subject at hand?" Robert asked. He grabbed Mona's hand. "I want to marry this filly as soon as possible."

Dexter looked astonished. "Robert, you're starting to talk like a Kentuckian."

Mona smiled at Robert and squeezed his

hand. "We'll get through this. We always do." She turned to Dexter, "I will be at the office at three. I want to hear what the staff has to say."

"That's not a good idea. Your presence will discourage them from speaking freely."

"I'll be in the next room with the door open a tad. They won't know I'm even there."

"You'll keep quiet? Not say a word."

Mona crossed her heart. "Quiet as a mouse."

"I'm going to visit those two miscreant solicitors as soon as they get settled," Robert said.

"I wish you wouldn't, Robert. You have a volatile temper. Let me handle this for you," Dexter advised.

"I have an idea," Willie offered. "Let's quit talking about this. It will get straightened out."

Mona laughed. "Oh, goodness, so sorry, Willie. We're boring you to tears with this nonsense."

"I'm not crying yet, but I shall be soon. This event is just a little bump in the road."

Mona nodded, but wasn't so sure.

Sometimes those bumpy roads cave in and make going forward impossible.

9

Mona sat where she could see the interviewee and hear without being seen.

The staff came in one-by-one to be questioned by Dexter. He allowed his fastest stenographer to take notes of the discussions. As soon as a staff member was interviewed, Dexter let them go home to their families. Almost everyone had heard of the murder and was aghast at the seriousness of the situation. It looked bad for Moon Enterprises and Mona since everyone knew or guessed why the three British lawyers were here.

Mona winced at the association. It was still a man's world, and a woman's reputation marked her path in life. She took exception that nothing untoward was inferred to Robert's character.

The afternoon dragged on until early evening. It didn't look like anyone knew anything of importance about the three British lawyers until one of the Moon Enterprises junior attorneys stepped into the adjoining room. He was perspiring though the day had cooled, and the pallor of his complexion belied his discomfort.

Mona heard Dexter say, "Are you ill, Isom? You don't look well."

The young man threw himself into the chair before Dexter. "No, sir. I feel fine."

Mona noticed that he would not look Dexter in the eye.

Dexter must have noticed it, too. "Isom, I asked you to drop off the British gentlemen to their hotel."

"Yes, sir."

"Did you?"

"Yes, sir."

"What was the conversation in the car?"

"They didn't say much, sir. I pointed out items of interest and dropped them off."

"It's only three blocks to the hotel."

Isom nodded and patted the sweat off his upper lip with his handkerchief.

"Did you take them on a little sightseeing tour?"

Isom took a few seconds to answer. "They wanted to see something of the town."

"Where did you take them?"

"Around Gratz Park, Transylvania University, and the University of Kentucky."

"Did you point out Belle Brezing's house?"

Isom nodded. "I thought nothing of it, sir."

"Did you take them to Belle Brezing's house?"

Isom's eyes lit up. "No, sir. I did not. I took them to their hotel and let them out at the front door. They went straight inside."

"Did you accompany them?"

"No, sir. I came back to the office and worked for another hour."

Dexter knew that was true as it checked out with information gathered from the rest of the staff.

"Did you go with them to Belle Brezing's house that evening?"

"No, sir. I was with my girl at the picture show. I never saw them again after I dropped them off at their hotel."

"Where did you go after the picture show?"

"I walked my girl home, had a piece of apple pie in her mother's kitchen, and then went home to bed."

"Did any of the Brits indicate they wanted to visit the red-light district?"

"No, sir. They never commented on it."

"Not one?"

"No, sir. I swear."

"Do you know anything that can throw light on why the Brits went to Belle Brezing's house and the subsequent murder?"

"No, sir. Nothing."

Dexter looked at the stenographer. "Get all that?"

"Yes, sir."

Satisfied, Dexter said to the young man, "You may leave now."

Isom stood, holding his hat. "Mr. Deatherage, am I fired?"

Dexter gathered his notes. "No, Isom, but . . ."

"Yes, sir?"

"If I hear a whisper of you ever visiting a bawdy house yourself, your career with Moon

Enterprises will come to an abrupt end."

Isom swallowed. "No, sir. I mean, yes, sir. I won't, sir. You have my word."

"You're dismissed."

Isom exited the office so fast, the stenographer laughed.

Dexter chuckled himself. "Do you think I put the fear of God into that young man?"

The stenographer nodded. "He'll think twice before getting into mischief, Mr. Deatherage."

Mona didn't agree.

She thought Isom was lying.

10

"Has everyone been interviewed?" Mona asked.

"We have one more person—the new attorney I hired to submit our mining patents."

"It's getting late. When's he coming in?"

"He should have been here by now, Mona. Let me call and see if he's been detained." Dexter went into the switchboard room and called the young man's home.

Mona listened to the conversation and became somewhat alarmed when Dexter repeated, "You said he left an hour ago for the office? Well, he's not here. Do you know where he could have gone?"

Mona could tell from Dexter's expression that he was perplexed.

He hung up the receiver. "Excuse me for a moment. Stay here, please." Dexter checked the hallway, reception area, and the rest of the offices. Besides himself and Mona, no one was in the Moon Enterprises offices, except for two Pinkertons cooling their heels by the elevator.

Perplexed, Dexter returned to Mona. "Hancock Jeter is not here. His wife said he left over an hour ago."

"What does he do here?"

"He's a new attorney I hired to submit our mining patents and claims."

Mona felt alarmed. "Let's take a look at his office, Dexter."

"I checked. He's not there."

"Let's go through his desk. I've got a bad feeling about this."

Mona and Dexter went to Hancock's office, where she noticed a safe in the corner. "Do you have the combination?"

"Yes, it's where we store the drawings and copies of the schematics for the Moon patents."

"Claim applications, too?"

"You betcha."

"Why is the safe here?"

"It was more convenient for the attorney taking care of these issues than to run down to the bank where we have a deposit box."

"Who has keys to the deposit box?"

"Just the bank manager and myself."

"What's in the deposit box?"

"Copies of everything pertaining to the patents and claims."

"Who has access to this safe?"

"I have the combination. Also, my personal secretary and Hancock. That's it."

"You have a safe in your office. What's in there?"

"Personal papers of the Moon family—wills, birth certificates, property deeds, marriage licenses, letters of instructions in case of death, etc. I'm the only one who has access to that safe."

"Dexter, open the safe, please."

Dexter dialed the combination for the safe and pulled out files and drawings. He laid them on a large table and went through them carefully while Mona checked Mr. Jeter's desk. She slumped into his chair after an exhaustive search even pulling out drawers and checking underneath them.

"Nothing," Mona said with exasperation. "No checkbook, no hidden bottle of booze, no indiscreet love letters, nothing. In fact, this desk is too neat and orderly. Doesn't even look like anyone works from it."

Dexter sheepishly looked up. "I've got some bad news. Two patents for a new drilling rig are missing."

"That's not good." Mona thought for a moment. "Do you have a picture of this Hancock Jeter?"

"Yes, with his employee file."

"Can you get it, please? I'll make a call to the Pinkerton boys at home and have them search for Mr. Jeter, but they'll need that picture."

"Mona, have one of them watch the Jeter house, too."

Mona tried to use the phone. She was perplexed when the phone had no dial tone. After all, Dexter had just made a call. "How do I call out?"

"I'll make the call. I know how to use the switchboard. Mona, go home. I've got lots to do."

"And I'm in the way."

Dexter nodded. "Sorry, but I've got to move fast. I'll be in touch when I find something out."

"Okay. I'll be at home." Mona left Dexter busily going through files and summoned the two Pinkertons waiting in the hallway. "I'm going to the Phoenix Hotel and then home. Jamison will take me. You stay here with Mr. Deatherage. He will have instructions for you."

Knowing it was no use to argue with their employer, they agreed. "Yes, Miss Moon."

Mona left the offices of Moon Enterprises feeling gloomy. Not only was the murder hanging over her head, but also a possible theft of important patents involving one missing Moon attorney.

Where was Hancock Jeter?

11

Mona's driver, Jamison, let Mona off the hotel's front door.

An attendant opened the car door.

Before exiting her new black Ford Deluxe, Mona said to Jamison, "I shan't be long."

Jamison then went to park the car where he could see the comings and goings of the hotel. He knew Miss Mona would want to know the foot traffic around the hotel. Mona might be a few minutes or she might be hours, so he settled in his seat, thankful he had a thermos of hot coffee and a piece of cinnamon coffee cake with him.

Mona entered the lobby and handed a note to a desk clerk. "I'll be waiting in the mezzanine lobby."

The clerk looked at the note. "I don't know if he's in." He stared at Mona and waited.

Getting the message, Mona slipped him a fin. "The mezzanine lobby. Immediately." She climbed the short flights of steps to the mezzanine and eased into a green, leather wingback chair, picked up a Ladies' Home Journal magazine, and thumbed through it.

Ten minutes later Jellybean Martin, dressed as a waiter, emerged from the service elevator with a tray holding a cocktail. The small, almost dwarfish man placed a napkin before Mona and placed a drink on it. He also left a small bowl of peanuts. Quietly he murmured, "How did you know I still worked here?"

"I took a chance. I need help, Jellybean."

"Payment?"

"Fifty dollars for a few hours work."

Jellybean's eyes lit up. "What do you need?"

"I want you to ask around the hotel about the three Brits who were staying here."

"What do you want to know about them?"

"Now I know you have already heard that one of them got stabbed at Belle Brezing's place. Don't play dumb with me."

Jellybean grinned. "You came to the right

man. Give me a few hours."

"Don't call. Come to Moon Manor."

"I don't have a car."

"I'll have my man bring you out. He'll be waiting for you at the employee's entrance."

"Have him come for me in four hours. I have contacts in Belle's kitchen. I want to hear what they've got to say."

The elevator door opened and a guest stepped out.

Jellybean said in a loud, sloppy voice. "I hope you enjoy your Mint Julep, miss. We put in extra, extra bourbon just like you asked."

The departing guest shot Mona a strange look and, thinking twice before waiting in the mezzanine lobby, went down the staircase.

Mona took a quick sip of the Mint Julep before picking up her purse.

"Remember, four hours. My shift ends then."

"My man will be here. You better be, too."

"For fifty dollars, you bet I will. I want that in cash. No check."

Mona said, "As you wish." There was chattering coming up the stairs, so Mona went down the other side of the double staircase.

When she glanced back, Jellybean was gone.

12

Mona barely made it home in time for dinner. She ran upstairs to change when she bumped into Violet waiting at the top of the staircase. "Excuse me, Violet. I've got to change. Robert will be here any second."

"I need to talk with you, Miss Mona."

Mona looked at Violet's anxious face. She could see that Violet had been crying. "Oh, goodness, Violet. Come and help me dress. Tell me all about it." Mona took a key from her purse and unlocked her bedroom door, which was always kept locked.

Violet followed Mona into the lavish bedroom suite and watched Mona kick off her shoes and throw her hat and gloves on the bed. Mona quickly slipped off her dress and put on a robe.

"Sit," Mona said, pointing to a chair before the marble fireplace. After sitting herself, Mona leaned forward and clasped Violet's hands. "Now—what has happened?"

"You know that Jacob Gentry goes my church?"

Mona nodded.

"That awful man was spreading the worst gossip about you after church. He called you a Jezebel and said that you needed to be run out of the county or worse. Mr. Gentry was getting people all riled up saying that you owned bawdy houses in Lexington and that's how Moon Enterprises made its money and that you were probably a . . ." Violet hung her head.

"Go on, Violet."

Violet lifted her head with tears in her eyes. "He said you were probably a harlot yourself before you came here."

Mona was taken aback. Stunned was more the word for it. "Did Gentry say how he was making this connection?"

Violet whispered, "Because of that British lawyer who was found dead at Belle Brezing's house. Everyone knows they came because of Lord Farley."

"We're supposed to call Lord Farley 'His Grace' now," Mona said absent-mindedly.

"What?"

Mona waved her hand. "Oh, nothing, Violet. Did people believe Gentry?"

"Yes. That's what's got me so worried. You should have seen people's faces—so ugly. The locals are angry about the wages you pay your employees, and the fact you are so successful. Men don't like a woman being successful."

"Men in charge seldom do. They don't want to share their wealth, even if it means one penny out of their pocket. That's what's ruining this country—selfishness and stupidity."

There was a knock on the door. Dora called out, "Miss Mona, His Grace is here."

"I'll be down in a moment, Dora."

"Thank you, miss."

Mona turned her attention to her maid. "Dry your tears, Violet and don't mention this to the rest of the staff."

"Aren't you worried, Miss Mona?"

"Yes, but right now I'm going to dress for dinner with my beau. Have you had dinner yet?"

"I don't see how you can be so calm, after all

the good things you have done for our community. People are so ungrateful. I'm so mad it makes
my blood boil."

"I think you need a hot meal and a good
night's sleep. Things will look better in the
morning."

Violet didn't believe Mona's words, but said,
"Yes, miss."

"Go downstairs and tell Robert I'll be a few
moments and then have Monsieur Bisaillon fix
you a plate. I know there is chocolate cake left
over from lunch." When Violet hesitated, Mona
said, "You're dismissed, young lady. Get something to eat. Go on now."

Violet slowly left the room, giving Mona one
last look.

Mona was sure Violet was holding something
back.

She had the same feeling as with Isom.

There were unspoken truths.

13

Mona and Robert said very little during dinner. They certainly couldn't speak of the murder with the servants always listening. Not that the staff meant any harm, but their identity and much of their self-worth were reliant upon the fortunes of Moon Manor and Moon Enterprises. Of course, they were interested.

After dinner, Mona had dessert and coffee served by the pool. After Samuel placed the tray on the garden table, Mona waited several minutes before speaking. "Do you think we're alone now?"

"To be sure, let's turn the chairs away from the house. I swear Samuel can read lips."

Mona chuckled. "I have to agree my staff is a nosey bunch."

"How did the interviews go?"

"Hasn't Dexter called you?"

"No."

"It seems one of my attorneys is missing along with two patent designs."

Robert replied, "Ouch."

"That's what I say."

"Is it connected to the murder?"

Mona said, "Don't know, darling. I hope not."

"What a mess."

"What about Mr. Dankworth and his associate?"

Robert rubbed his chin with his thumb. "They are sitting tight in one of my workers' bungalows. I haven't talked to them yet."

"How are they eating?"

"One of your Pinkertons bought groceries and is keeping an eye on them. I have sent word that I will fire them and offer no letter of recommendation if they don't cooperate. That should make them quake in their boots."

"And they offered any explanation?"

"Not to me yet, but I'm going to see them first thing tomorrow. Should get some answers then."

"I doubt they will be forthcoming."

"Maybe, but we have another problem."

Mona threw up her hands in despair. "What!"

"The papers are going forth with the murder story tomorrow."

"Are we going to be named?"

"Don't know yet, but steel yourself for the backlash. Sooner or later our connection will come out."

"What about national papers?"

"It will be picked up by the Associated Press if our names are connected. And if that happens, it will make international news. I am so sorry, Mona. I feel like this is my fault. If my solicitors hadn't come to the States, none of this would have happened."

"I thought they were Brynelleth's solicitors."

"Too late for distinction now."

"Yes, it is. People always look at the broad strokes during a scandal." Mona gave a small sigh and decided not to tell Robert about Jacob Gentry and his insinuations. "Well, we'll just have to make the best of it."

"I think Willie was right."

"About what?"

"Let's throw an engagement party," Robert suggested.

"I can't think of a worse time for a party. We haven't settled the dispute over inheritance or who lives where."

"I'll settle it right now. You live six months at Brynelleth and six months here. I'll be here when I can. The first born son gets Brynelleth and has my last name. The first born daughter has the Moon moniker and gets Moon Enterprises."

"What if the first born is a daughter?"

Frustrated, Robert growled, "What if we have all sons or all daughters? Work with me, Mona, for God's sakes."

Mona laughed.

Robert's brow tightened before he broke out with a grin. "Oh, I see. You were teasing."

"This won't be an easy marriage, Robert. I hope you understand that. Don't expect me to be a humdrum wife."

"If you were going to be a fuddy-duddy, I wouldn't want you as my wife." Robert reached over and pulled Mona out of her chair to his lap. "Come here," he said in a low, husky voice, wrapping his arms around her.

Mona recognized the desire in Robert's voice.

"You sure you don't want to run away to Italy and forget about all this?"

Mona kissed Robert's cheek before laying her head on his shoulder. "Sounds pretty tempting, doesn't it? How about we go to Italy on our honeymoon?"

"Is that where you want to go?"

"I have a hankering to see great art, eat lots of pasta, and swim in the Mediterranean. Where did you want to go?"

"Kenya."

"That sounds interesting as well. Or we could go out west."

Robert kissed the top of Mona's head. "Never been there."

"Ahem," Mr. Thomas said, looking discreetly away from the romantic couple. "So sorry to bother you, miss."

Robert jumped up and deposited Mona on her feet. "Bloody hell, man. Can't we ever get a moment to ourselves?"

Ignoring Robert's tirade, Mr. Thomas said, "Mr. Deatherage is on the phone and says it is most urgent that he speak with you."

Mona smoothed down her dress. "Oh, dear. Another fire I suppose. I wonder what has happened now." She turned to Robert. "I'm going to talk with Dexter and then call it a night."

Robert frowned. "Breakfast tomorrow?"

"I'll call, Robert. I may be frightfully busy."

"Alright, dear," Robert said, kissing Mona on the cheek. "I'll be at home if you need me."

Mona hurried inside while Robert watched her leave.

Before Mr. Thomas followed, he gave Robert a look of disdain.

Robert was aghast. Servants in his world did not offer opinions if they wanted to keep their jobs. A good servant was never noticed by members of Robert's class. He had to admit he didn't know the names of all the staff at Brynelleth.

He could not deny things were different in the United States. Moon Manor's employees were devoted to Mona, and she was especially close to Mr. Thomas. Even though they were of a different gender, generation, and race, they had much in common. Both had to scramble to get where they were in life and had met with much discrimination, cruelty, and heartache on the way.

It never occurred to Robert to consider that Mona's employees might disapprove of him. After all, he was a duke—a nobleman descended from a king. They were just lowborn servants. So, why did Mr. Thomas' condemnation rattle him so? Robert knew it was because he respected Mr. Thomas, the son of a slave, and it bothered him that Thomas did not reciprocate.

Robert would have to make it right with Mr. Thomas.

14

Mona picked up the phone. "What's happened?"

Dexter said, "The story will hit the papers tomorrow with Robert listed in connection."

"Surely, they won't insinuate that he had anything to do with them being at Brezing's place or the murder."

"You know how people's minds work. They'll put two and one together and come up with four."

"Poor Robert." Mona felt sick to her stomach.

"Poor you. You are guilty by association. I've already had calls from members of the Moon Enterprises board and your Aunt Melanie. She is stirring things up and wants you removed as head."

"There is no legal way she can do that."

"Maybe not, but she can sue you as morally unfit and ruin your reputation."

"Is she threatening that?"

"Hinting at it."

"All she wants is money. Let's call her bluff."

"I don't know, Mona. She's got a lot of ammunition this time."

"Well, stall her as long as you can."

"Will try."

"Okay, keep me posted. Talk to you tomorrow." Mona hung up and resisted the urge to call Robert, thinking he should have one last night of peaceful sleep.

Bone tired, Mona had to stay up. She rang for Samuel.

Appearing in the library, he asked, "Yes, miss?"

"Samuel, I'm going to have a visitor later tonight. Jamison will bring him to the front door. Have the visitor stay in the car. Just come and get me."

"Yes, miss."

"And Samuel—you are not to discuss this visit with anyone. Even Mr. Thomas."

"I understand."

"Bring me a pot of hot coffee. Is there any chocolate cake left?"

"No, but Monsieur Bisaillon made an apple pie for tomorrow's lunch."

"Cut me a large slice of that, please."

"Chef will be mad."

"Chef Bisaillon is always mad. Please bring it. Thank you, Samuel."

"Yes, miss."

Mona turned to paperwork she had neglected and glancing at the clock, waited for the sound of her car returning.

15

Samuel shook Mona's shoulder.

She groggily lifted her head from the desk. "Oh, I fell asleep."

"Jamison is outside."

"Good. Very good. I want you to leave the kitchen door open and go to bed, Samuel. And I mean—to bed. I'll lock up."

Perturbed, Samuel did as Mona bid. He wanted to see who was in the car.

Mona patted her hair and went to the front door. She quietly opened it and went down the limestone steps to where Jamison was waiting.

"Go to the kitchen and get something to eat. Don't wake anyone up, Jamison."

"I'll be quiet, miss."

"There's a nice apple pie on the counter. Take

as much as you want."

"Fresh milk in the icebox?"

"Help yourself. I'll come and get you when I'm finished. Go around to the back."

Jamison grinned before he scampered off. It has been a long time since he had a slice of apple pie, and it sounded very appealing.

Mona got into the car and drove off in the direction of the horse barns.

"Where are we going?" asked Jellybean, amused at Mona's shenanigans.

"To where my prying employees can't hear us."

She stopped the car before a white-fenced meadow. "What did you find out?"

"Not much. I talked to all hotel staff. The Brits were considered nuisances—always complaining about this and that."

"Like what?"

"The rooms were too warm. The service too slow. That type of thing."

"It is a very warm summer. They are not used to such heat in Britain."

"Hmm."

"Can you tell me something useful—like did

they speak with anyone? Did anyone visit them? Did they ask where they could find 'gentlemen's entertainment?'"

"They transferred in Cincinnati from the New York train to Lexington on Thursday. They were not in the hotel much of Friday or Saturday morning. No one knew exactly where they went as a driver picked them up and returned them each time in the same car."

"Was it the same man who drove?" Mona knew that Dexter had selected the two new Moon attorneys to escort the Brynelleth men about town. Could someone else have co-opted them?

"The doorman doesn't think so, but couldn't give a description."

"What else?"

"They had Friday and Saturday breakfast at the hotel and dinner for Thursday, Friday, and Saturday. They were unhappy with the Saturday menu and complained of being hungry."

"What time did they leave the hotel?"

"The night doorman says around nine in the evening."

"All three together?"

"That's what he said."

"Could he be lying?"

"Of course. Everyone could be lying."

"No one at the hotel suggested visiting a bordello—doorman, bellhop, bartender, waiter?"

"No one is going to admit that, Miss Mona."

"Is that all?"

"Yep, that about sums it up."

"Got any ideas?"

"I think the young gentleman would not pay the lady's price, and she gave him the what for."

"She has an alibi, Jellybean."

"Who would believe a bunch of whores and gamblers?"

"The coroner, that's who. The lady in question has a rock solid alibi, and it coincides with the time of death." Mona started the car again. "Do you know Belle Brezing?"

"Not very well. I have a cousin who works there off and on, so I've talked to Miss Belle a few times."

"What's she like?"

Jellybean pondered for a moment. "She's an old lady now, but still spry. Reads a lot. Drinks. Follows the ponies. Keeps her hand in the prostitution game for old friends. Has a couple of girls, but very limited goings-on there in that regard. Mostly stays out of the public eye. I'm sure she is not happy that this death has thrust her upon the national stage again, being that this is her second murder."

"What do you mean, Jellybean?"

"When Belle was fifteen, she got pregnant and married a man by the name of James Kenney. He worked with Johnny Cook, who was a good friend of Belle's and many think this Cook was in love with Belle."

"So why didn't she marry Cook?"

"Don't know. Nobody knows, but Johnny Cook was found on Jefferson Street with a bullet hole in his head and a message from Belle in his pocket."

Mona was spellbound. "The message?"

"Something about getting her a gun. This was only nine days after she had been married."

"She kill Johnny Cook?"

"Don't know. Don't even know if she was interviewed by the police."

Mona knew where her duty lay. She had to see this Belle Brezing. "I want you to give her this note as soon as possible." Mona handed him a note with a wax seal.

"What's in it?"

"You never mind. Just deliver it."

Jellybean whistled. "You want to see her? Is this a request for an audience with the notorious Belle Brezing? I just told you what kind of woman she was."

"Just deliver it, Jellybean. Here's twenty-five dollars."

"You said fifty," Jellybean protested.

"When you give me another twenty-five dollars worth of information, you'll get the rest."

Jellybean snorted in derision.

"Cheer up, Jellybean. It takes you a week to earn twenty-five dollars minus tips at the hotel. You'll get your other twenty-five as soon as you dig up some more information."

"Have it your way."

Mona stopped the car at the kitchen door.

Jamison was waiting for her and left with Jellybean munching on a slice of apple pie that the chauffeur had procured for him.

Mona locked the back door and cut two more slices of pie—one for herself and another piece for Violet, who she knew would still be awake waiting for her. Putting a pitcher of cold milk, two glasses, and the pie on a tray, Mona hurried to her bedroom.

Monsieur Bisaillon would be furious in the morning when he discovered his apple pie had been eaten during the night.

That would teach him to leave a pie out to cool on the kitchen counter!

16

Robert strolled to the back of his property where several small bungalows for farm workers were clustered.

Dexter walked by his side along with a stenographer, who was dismayed that her leather shoes were getting wet from the tall grass.

The two men climbed the stairs of one bungalow while the stenographer waited. Robert knocked on the door.

Mr. Dankworth answered. "Your Grace," he said, bowing his head.

Robert pushed past him into the room that served as both a living room and kitchen. Dexter followed along with the stenographer. She set up her equipment on the kitchen table and pulled up a chair.

"We'll interview you first," Robert said to Dankworth. "Where's the other fellow?"

"Mr. Madgwick is taking a stroll."

"Your instructions were to stay inside."

"It's so stuffy in here."

"Open a window," Robert said, exasperated. He was very cross with the solicitors.

"Mr. Dankworth, pull up a chair," Dexter advised. "We'll worry about Mr. Madgwick later. Robert, sit down, please."

"First, I would like to apologize for this appalling situation in which we have placed you," Dankworth said to Robert, who didn't reply.

"Let's start at the beginning, shall we?" Dexter said. "Remember, in the States, this is considered an affidavit. Do you understand, Mr. Dankworth?"

"Yes, let us proceed."

Dexter nodded to the stenographer.

She turned her machine on.

"Mr. Dankworth, you are the senior head of a three solicitor team from Brynelleth who has come to negotiate the hereditary rights of future children before the marriage of Duke Lawrence Robert Emerton Dagobert Farley to a Miss Mona

Moon. Is that correct?"

"It is. I am employed by the Brynelleth estate and not Robert Farley personally."

"But your job is to protect the interests of the current duke of Brynelleth and his future progeny?"

"Yes, if that means protecting the assets of Brynelleth."

"Even when that is at odds with His Grace's wishes?"

"His Grace's father always followed my advice. There was never a problem."

"You say you are a solicitor."

"Yes, I handle wills, legal transactions, and so forth. If a matter goes to trial, a barrister is hired. Solicitors do not speak in court."

"I see. Does Brynelleth have a barrister on retainer?"

"Our last barrister, Mr. Haeg, passed away, and the estate has not needed to hire another."

Dexter nodded. "You arrived in Lexington late Thursday. Can you share your schedule with us?"

"A Moon motorcar picked us at the railway station and took us to the hotel. We slept late the next day as we were very tired coming all the way from England. We had an afternoon appointment with you and were scheduled to meet with Miss Moon the following morning. On Saturday, we finished our meetings in the early afternoon, and your man Isom drove us back to our hotel."

"Isom just drove you to your hotel?"

"He gave us a brief tour about town before taking us to the hotel."

"Did that tour include the red-light district?"

Mr. Dankworth looked embarrassed. "No, sir, it did not."

Dexter continued his questioning. "Did you or the other two solicitors ask Isom to drive through the red-light district?"

"No, sir. We did not."

"What happened on Saturday night?"

"The three of us were having dinner at the hotel when your young attorney, Mr. Hancock Jeter joined us.

"Was he invited?"

"No, he showed up unexpectedly."

"Then what happened?"

"He said he was checking on us and were we happy?"

Dankworth offered, "I said we were not. The food at the hotel was awful. The rolls were soggy, the fish overcooked, and the soup cold. That's not to mention the watered down cocktails and no wine list."

"He said he knew where we could dine with pleasure and the liquor flowed like water. Mr. Madgwick stated that it was after nine, and it was his observation that the sidewalks rolled up at eight. Jeter said he knew of a men's club that was open 24/7 and they served the best food in town."

"We asked him to make a call to see if they would receive us and he did. We reached the establishment by nine thirty."

"How did you get there?"

"We walked. It was only a few blocks from the hotel."

"Then what?"

"We had a fine dinner of filet of sole, roasted potatoes, broccoli casserole, a hearty bean soup with fresh homemade rolls slathered with thick butter washed down by lots of your local bour-bon."

"And you didn't realize you were in a bordel-lo?"

"No, sir. Not at first. We were introduced to prominent men from the community who were playing card games or billiards. Everything was proper. No one cursed or discussed women. We didn't even see loose women at first. All the servants were men except for the maid who answered the door."

Robert interjected, "How pedestrian."

"I like billiards, so I played a few games and then joined the others playing bridge."

"Bridge?" asked Dexter.

"Yes, bridge. Then some of the men broke off and began playing poker. I joined in."

Dexter looked in disbelief at Robert. "Then what?"

"I got caught up in poker and was winning, so I didn't want to go. Madgwick fell asleep on a couch. Jones played billiards and drank. It wasn't until several young ladies came downstairs much later in the evening that I understood where I was."

"Why didn't you and the others leave immediately?"

Dankworth hung his head in shame. "Because I was on a lucky streak. I was winning a lot of money. If I had gathered the young lads and made them come with me, Jones would not be dead now."

Robert asked, "He was the only one of you three who went upstairs for other amusement?"

"Yes, both Madgwick and I are married. Jones is single and young. Surely you must understand."

"What happened then?" Dexter asked.

"It got very late. Madgwick and I went back to the hotel."

"Without the young Mr. Jones?"

"That's right, Mr. Deatherage. We didn't know anything about the murder until the next morning when Sheriff Monahan pounded on our door."

"Where was Mr. Jeter all this time?"

"He escorted us to the house, went inside with us, and then disappeared. I never saw him again."

"Did he have dinner with you?"

"No, sir. He excused himself and went down a back hallway. That's the last I saw of him. I don't know about Madgwick. Maybe he saw Jeter later."

Dexter said, "I thought the two of you stayed together."

"We did have to use the gents, sir. You didn't expect us to escort each other to the washroom."

"How many times did you use the washroom?"

Dankworth looked disgusted. "Really, sir. Most unseemly."

"How many times?"

"Three, maybe. Whiskey goes right through me."

"What about Madgwick?"

Dankworth bristled. "How would I know? Much of the night is a blur, but I did win at poker. Next morning I found a wad of cash in my pocket."

Robert was most disturbed.

Dankworth continued. "I was awakened by Sheriff Monahan and taken to jail where I was thrown in the drunk tank as he so aptly named it."

Robert said, "I got the idea you were taken by Monahan at Brezing's house."

"No, sir. Madgwick and I were at the hotel. We were awakened at eight in the morning and taken to jail."

"Were you still drunk?" Deatherage asked bluntly.

"I was. I don't know about Madgwick."

"Did the sheriff say why you were being apprehended?"

"Not at first. Only when we reached the jail, did the sheriff tell us the reason why."

"Do you have any other information?"

"Not that I can remember at the moment, Mr. Deatherage." He turned to Robert. "Am I still employed, Your Grace? I have a wife and two daughters. I am their sole support."

"You and Madgwick are going to meet with Miss Moon and give her everything she wants in writing. If you don't, I will fire you both without a letter of recommendation."

"But sir?"

"Without my blessing, no one will hire you."

Dankworth nodded, knowing he was beaten. He feared that the Brynelleth estate would fall into the hands of Americans and be lost to English descendants forever. Foreigners were purchasing the old estates at an alarming rate. He thought it would be the ruin of Great Britain as he believed in the proper order of people and property. People should know their place. He feared Mona Moon did not and her ideas of where she thought she belonged in the pecking order of the world frightened him. "I will need a typewriter, a notary republic, and a telephone, sir. Also, someone who can take dictation."

Deatherage replied, "I will make sure you have the use of my office and equipment. It will have to be after office hours as I don't want others to see you. I want everyone to think you have gone back to Great Britain."

"Very good, sir." All smugness and superiority had drained from Dankworth. He looked like a defeated man. Even the skin on his cheeks looked shrunken.

Robert said, coldly, "Please wait outside and send in Madgwick."

"Yes, Your Grace." Dankworth rubbed his sweating hands on his pants before standing to fetch Madgwick. He walked out of the room a shaken person.

Robert took a deep breath. "This is awful bullying a man like Dankworth. He's a good chap. Did you know he lost a son in the Great War?"

"He's a man whose time has passed him by, but he doesn't know it," Deatherage said.

"Dankworth believes the sun still does not set on the British Empire. He doesn't realize the British Empire is no longer the top dog. Your empire is falling apart. It won't be long before India pulls away."

"The sun never sets on the British Empire," Robert whispered. "I once fought for that."

"Do you still believe in king and country?"

"I don't know what I believe in, Dexter. I came away from the muddy trenches in France so disillusioned. I lost hope until I met Mona. I wish I could be more like her. Mona believes she can change the world for the better."

Dexter said, "Maybe Mona will. She's got the money and the power to do so."

"Not if she marries me. I'll clip her wings. I know I will."

"Look at all the good she's done in the Bluegrass."

"And Mona's hated for it. She is labeled as an activist—a progressive of the worst kind. I've even heard some claim that she is a Communist. Local fat cats are always nipping at her heels—always working to pull her down. I was taught noblesse oblige—the rich and powerful have an obligation to those less fortunate. I understand what Mona is reaching for."

"Then let's work to protect her—watch her back. I believe in Mona," Dexter declared. "I intend to go all the way with her."

"Is that your moral compass talking or the considerable salary Mona pays you?"

Dexter grinned. "Both, my good man. I am a practical man. If I can help Mona change the world while receiving my retainer, I'll do it. I'm no saint."

"Neither am I, and that's the problem."

"Perhaps Mona needs someone to advise her not to reach for the moon all the time."

"You tell her. I'm not going to have my head bitten off." Robert leaned back in his chair. "Let's get this last interview over with. I want to see Mona."

Dexter checked his notes. "She's not home."

"Where is she?"

"She went into town."

"To do what?"

Dexter readied himself for the explosion that would occur. "She went to have morning tea with Miss Brezing. She's at Belle's."

17

Two Pinkertons dropped Mona off at Belle Brezing's house and parked in the alley behind the house per Mona's instructions. She was wearing a solid black dress, including a hat with a long widow's veil.

The housekeeper, Pearl, who must have been watching the street, opened the front door as soon as Mona stepped on the landing. Mona was ushered in quickly. The music of Bessie Smith softly drifted down the staircase. Mona glanced upstairs, but saw no one as she was ushered into Miss Belle's private parlor. It smelled heavily of cigarette smoke, spilled whiskey, and sour milk, not to mention filled with knickknacks. There was not a space on a table, mantel, or shelf that was not covered in hand-crocheted doilies or porcelain statues of shepherdesses being courted by the young sons of noblemen.

On the wall was a photograph of Brezing as a young woman standing in this very room in front of a table laden with the finest linens, crystal, and china with middle-aged men in formal attire sitting around it. Mona studied their faces, but didn't recognize anyone. There was a plaque attached to the photograph that stated *Opening Night 1891.* That was way before Mona's time and she concluded that most of the men had passed on by now. She wondered if they had been guests or investors into Brezing's business. Even though the parlor was too dark and "Victorian" for her taste, Mona was astonished at the number of books lying about. Pulling the black lace from her hat, Mona looked at several old spines. She picked up a copy of Dickens' *David Copperfield* and inspected it.

"That's a first edition."

Mona swirled to see an old woman wearing black also with the skirt to her ankles. She leaned on a cane. Her once glorious red hair was now gray and her face was heavily lined. Her hands trembled a bit.

"Miss Brezing?"

"Call me Belle please. Like I was saying, that is a first edition. I have many first editions in my collection—Mark Twain, Oscar Wilde, Charles Dickens, Jane Austen—even Proust."

"I see you like Zane Grey novels."

"I like to read westerns. Did you know Zane Grey was a dentist?"

"I did not."

"I like his books. Also quite fond of Irvin S. Cobb and O. Henry short stories. Have you read *The Ransom of Red Chief?* Very amusing." Arranging her long skirts, Brezing sat before the fireplace and extended her hand to a chair in front of her. "Please sit, my dear." She rang a bell.

A maid answered.

"Tea, please. And bring those new sugar biscuits."

"Yes, ma'am."

Mona sat down.

"Do you read, dear?"

"I'm afraid I am addicted to English mysteries."

"Do you like the male English writers or the females?"

"The women. I think they have more insight into the human heart while the male writers are more action oriented."

"So you read Agatha Christie and Dorothy L. Sayers. I am partial to Wilkie Collins myself."

Mona nodded, entranced by Brezing's dark eyes. They appeared as though they flashed every now and then.

"I suggest you read *The Maltese Falcon* by Dashiell Hammett. He is a superb author. Another favorite mystery writer is James M. Cain. He just released *The Postman Always Rings Twice*. Cain's books are more dramatic depicting the seamier side of crime, rather than mysteries. I think they are very true to life."

"Now that you mentioned crime, Miss Belle, I've come to ask a few questions, but first I want to thank you for seeing me. I haven't introduced myself. I am Mona Moon. I am Manfred Moon's niece."

Brezing interrupted. "I know who you are. I've heard quite a bit about you, my dear."

"Really? My name comes up in your establishment?"

"You'd be surprised how often. You have

apparently ruffled the feathers of several roosters around here. You pay black men the same wages as white men. That hits hard on a white man's ego. It goes against custom and tradition."

"I pay for the work. I don't care if a man is purple as long as he gets the job done."

There was a knock on the door, and the housekeeper entered with a tea tray. She laid it before the ladies on a hassock.

"That will be all, Pearl," Brezing said. "See that we are not disturbed." Brezing motioned to Mona. "Please pour, my dear. I have arthritis and my hands are stiff anymore."

Mona lifted the sterling silver teapot and poured the tea. "Sugar?"

"I take mine plain. No milk either."

Mona handed Brezing a Royal Doulton teacup, which she placed on a side table. "I'm here to find out what happened to Mr. Jones, the English solicitor."

"I gave my report to Sheriff Monahan."

"If you are anything like me, you always hold something back." Mona put down her cup. "Look, we are both business women in a man's world. We need to support each other."

Brezing scoffed. "Support each other? How you do go on, Miss Moon with your couture clothes and your white hair coifed into the latest style. You come around hiding under your mourning veil. I know you parked in the back of my house where no one could see your car. Here's how people like you *helped* me. I was twelve when I had my first sexual encounter. The man was thirty-six. Nothing happened to him, but I was ruined in society's eyes. A few years later, when I was at my mother's funeral, the landlord locked me out of our house and threw my possessions in the gutter. I had just given birth to a baby girl, so I went to work as a whore the next day. I was destitute, but needed to support my child. I didn't have the education nor the skills to be anything else. In that era, a woman could be married, a teacher, a cook, a dressmaker, or a prostitute. I don't regret what I am. I ran an honest house and made a good living. I still maintain a few girls for my older customers, but I've been retired to the public since before the Great War, so why are you bothering me?"

Mona asked tenderly, "What happened to your daughter, Miss Belle?"

Collecting her thoughts, Brezing hesitated before she spoke, "She was born spoiled and had to be placed in an institution. She's well taken care of."

"I'm so sorry."

Wondering why she confided this personal information to Mona, Brezing spat out, "I neither want nor need your pity, Miss Moon."

"I don't mean to be disrespectful, Miss Belle, but I need to know what happened the night Mr. Jones died. I might add that you're not the only woman who has been knocked around. I've had a few bruises myself."

Brezing smiled bitterly. "They said you had gumption." Brezing cocked her head to one side, studying Mona. "And you really do look like Jean Harlow. I've never seen anyone with your coloring."

"May we start over, Miss Belle?" Mona stuck out her hand. "Hello. I am Mona Moon. Pleased to meet you, and yes, I did wear a disguise to your house. I had my men park in the back, and I wore a veil so no one would recognize me. I'm sorry."

Brezing chuckled and shook Mona's hand. "You're not the first woman to sneak in my house wearing a veil, and you won't be the last. You have no idea how many wives have beseeched me to help with their husbands' gambling and drinking issues."

"Do you help?"

"I do what I can, especially if I know a man is throwing his career away or drinking himself to death. I hate to see a family ruined."

"That's why I'm here. This murder could have dire consequences to Moon workers. I employ thousands of men and a great deal of women, too. My aunt is trying to get me fired as head of Moon Enterprises."

"Can she do that?"

"Legally, no, but if she turns public opinion against me, I will be ineffective and will have to step down."

Brezing pondered for a moment. "My information is not free, you know."

Mona felt a chill. "What is your price?"

"I want you to come back on a regular basis, have tea, and discuss books with me. You look to be a reader, and I want someone to talk with who is not associated with my vocation."

Mona was flustered. She certainly didn't want

to offend this powerful woman, knowing that a whisper from her to one of her regular customers could cause trouble for Moon Enterprises. Mona decided to err on the side of politeness. "It would be my honor, but you should have tea at Moon Manor. I would love to show it to you."

"You say that now, but as soon as you are discovered visiting me by Lexington's good citizens, you'd be advised to prepare for the onslaught. It's best we keep our dealings discreet."

"Let's discuss compensation for your information later. Tell me what you know." Mona laid down her teacup. "Please, Miss Belle. My future could ride on what you tell me."

"The three English gentlemen came around nine-thirty. I saw them briefly before I retired to my library."

"Did you talk to them?"

"No, just saw them for a few seconds as my staff was taking their hats. I shut the door to my parlor and read for about an hour before going to bed."

"What happened then?"

"They had a good meal, drank a lot of my best

bourbon, played billiards, and then poker."

"All three of them played poker?"

"Only the older gentleman. One other played billiards until he fell asleep on the couch."

"What about Jones?"

"He went upstairs with my girl, Sally."

"Did she approach him or did he ask for her . . ." Mona searched for the correct word. "Companionship?"

"My girls never bring up the subject of sex, so Mr. Jones proposed to her."

"And?"

"Sally spent about an hour with the young man until he fell asleep. She then came down and spent the rest of the night talking with the other men and getting them drinks."

"What time did Sally come down?"

"She said it was about one in the morning."

"Who found Mr. Jones?"

"A cleaning maid."

"Pearl?"

"No, I have another gal come in early to change the bed linens and tidy the rooms."

"May I speak with her?"

"She's left town."

"How convenient."

"Isn't it though." Brezing held out the plate of sugar biscuits. "Cookie, Miss Moon?"

Mona took two sugar cookies and nibbled on one. "What is the unspoken truth, Miss Brezing? It seems like you're hinting at something."

"There was an argument between the two younger Englishmen over Sally. They both wanted her."

"Don't you have other ladies working for you?"

"These men both wanted Sally. I understand it had to do with her milk-white completion and red hair."

"How was the argument resolved?"

"Mr. Jones pushed the other gentleman to the floor and threatened him."

"I need this man's name. Was he part of the trio or another Englishmen who visited your house?"

"It was one of the three solicitors who came on behalf of Robert Farley to negotiate your marriage to him."

Surprised, Mona leaned back in her chair. "How did you know? Did they say that was their reason for being in Lexington?"

"Oh, my dear, besides peddling flesh, my other business is information. Men get a few drinks in them, and they will tell their deepest, darkest secrets to a pretty face."

"Again—did the Englishmen say they were here for Farley?"

"No, I heard that piece of gossip from my other girl."

Mona was aghast. If the solicitors didn't reveal the reason for their visit, that meant there was a leak somewhere else. Oh, goodness. "How did your girl come to that conclusion?"

"Jacob Gentry."

"How would she know Jacob Gentry?"

"He plays billiards here every Thursday night. He tells his wife that he is attending a Rotary Club meeting."

"I find that very interesting."

"I thought you would. Jacob Gentry doesn't like you." Brezing lit up a cigarette and inhaled. "In fact, he doesn't like women at all."

"Then what's he doing in a bawdy house?"

"The same as many men who come here. To make business deals, drink out of public view—

get away from their wives."

"Is that what he does?"

Brezing blew smoke through her nose before inhaling again. "Mainly Gentry gripes about the role of women in today's society. Like I said, he doesn't like us. Watch your back with that one. He's stirring people up about you and Farley."

"What's he saying?"

"That a woman who works in the public is wanton, and that you're not intelligent enough to run such a big company. The same excuses all men use to keep women in the kitchen and the bedroom."

Mona said, "I thought things would change once women got the right to vote."

"You must remember that Suffrage won because of a single vote. It was overwhelmingly voted against, and many men are working to overturn women's right to vote. There is a good chance the right-to-vote for women might become a thing of the past if these men get their way in Congress. It all starts at the grass-roots level though."

"I feel that you are trying to lead me in a certain direction, but I'm having trouble following the crumbs."

Brezing looked disappointed. "And I thought you were clever." She began coughing and looked about for a napkin.

Mona handed Brezing a handkerchief from her purse, after snatching the cigarette from the old woman's mouth and putting it out in a saucer. "Here. Drink some tea."

The madam drank some tea and leaned back in her chair, mopping her brow with Mona's handkerchief. "Thank you. You're very kind."

Mona stood. "I think I'd better be leaving. You are getting tired."

Brezing grabbed Mona's arm as she passed by. "If I were you, I'd investigate the relationship between Jacob Gentry and this girl. Maybe try the birth certificate office. Look about the year 1914."

"Which girl?"

"The girl no one wanted."

"What's this lady's name again?"

"Mira Hedge. Remember Mira Hedge. Remember—she's the woman no one wanted."

Mona thought that was a terrible thing to say about a person—the woman no one wanted.

She left Belle Brezing's house by the back

door and out through the gate to the alley where two Pinkertons were waiting. She stepped quickly into the car and only then did Mona lift her veil and breathe deeply.

One of the Pinkertons asked, "Where to, Miss Moon?"

"To the office, please. As fast as you can."

As the car drove out of the area, Mona glanced at two young women working a corner. In these hard times men, who lacked the where-with-all to feed their families, always had a few coins for these women.

Saddened at the sight of the prostitutes with their ruined stockings and thin cotton dresses, Mona murmured, "There but for the grace of God, go I."

18

"Have you sorted this mess out yet?" Mona asked Dexter. She was sitting in her sumptuous office located in the Moon Enterprises building downtown on Main Street.

"Still working on it," Dexter replied, lighting his pipe.

"Everyone is lying." Mona got up and opened a window to disperse the pipe smoke. The noise from street traffic sounded amidst the clattering sounds of typing coming from the outer secretarial pool.

Dexter chuckled. "You've noticed that, have you?"

"I went to see Belle Brezing today."

Dexter showed no emotion, except to blink several times. "How did that go?"

Mona sat behind her mahogany desk again. "She told me some surprising things."

Dexter leaned forward in his chair. "I'm all ears."

"Brezing said Jones and Madgwick got into a fight over a woman."

"Which woman?"

"The one that Jones ended up with—Sally. Here's another thing. Brezing said her maid found Jones, not this Sally person."

"Do tell?" Dexter pondered on this for a moment. "You're right. Witnesses are lying, which means there is guilt involved."

"We are going to have to dig deeper."

"Short of threatening people with a gun, I don't see how we can make people tell the truth. Do you think Brezing is selling you a story? She could be lying herself."

"For what purpose?"

"She could be protecting one of her girls. We have only her word that the maid found Jones."

"I would ask Sheriff Monahan, who told him that Jones was found by Sally. He may be making assumptions."

"I think we should stay as far away from Monahan as possible. It's not wise to go poking him."

Frustrated, Mona frowned. She wanted this murder investigation over and done with. "Have you ever been to Brezing's house?"

Dexter hesitated. "Once or twice."

Mona arched an eyebrow. "Did you meet Belle Brezing?"

"Once or twice."

"Come on Dexter. Give me the low-down," Mona coaxed.

"I was in her house years ago chasing down a creditor who owed your uncle money. I found him swilling down Brezing's gin and belting out *Danny Boy* while a ragtime record blared on the phonograph. Apparently, he was an old friend of Brezing."

"What did you think?"

"I thought it was a house stuck in time— around 1890."

"That's what I thought, too. It was clean, but smelled musty—like no one had aired it out for a long time. I'd like to get rid of all those tacky knickknacks in her library."

"Brezing's house closed down before the

Great War. After the war, other bawdy houses opened up again, but Brezing kept hers closed to the public. She only lets in friends and "friends" of friends. Her house is more like a private club now."

"She's an old woman. Maybe Brezing got tired of the hassle."

"Maybe."

"She told me something else."

"Yes?"

"Brezing said Jacob Gentry visits every Thursday evening when he is supposed to be at the Rotary Club."

Dexter broke out laughing. "That hypocritical old goat."

"She also told me to look for a connection between him and a Mira Hedge."

"Who is Mira Hedge?"

"The other witness who was at Brezing's the night Jones was murdered. She's the second lady in Brezing's employment."

"I'll get right on that."

"Any word about Hancock Jeter?"

"Nothing yet, but if he is within a hundred mile radius, we'll find him."

"Go talk to his wife again. Jeter might have been in touch with her since we last talked with her."

"Will do."

Ready to leave, Mona picked up her purse and gloves. "Did you ever get Uncle Manfred's money?"

Dexter stood and put out his pipe. "Nope. The man in question had blown it all on wine, women, and horses before I got to him."

"I'm curious. What did Uncle Manfred do?"

"He tore up the man's IOU. C'est la vie. You can't get blood from a rock."

"Maybe, but you can use that same rock to get someone else's blood. Depends on how you look at the problem."

Dexter escorted Mona out of the office and watched her walk down the hallway to the elevator—all the time wondering how far Mona would go to protect those she loved. The thought entered Dexter's mind that Mona would go all the way, and it made him shudder.

He hoped he never got in Mona's way.

19

Mona had started up the grand staircase when her secretary, Dotty, came out of Mona's home office.

"I need to see you right away, Mona," Dotty said.

Mona sighed. "Okay. Let me freshen up and I'll be straight down."

"I need to see you now. This can't wait."

Mona looked down from the staircase upon Dotty's concerned face. Noting that she was not going to take *no* for an answer, Mona relented and followed her into the office. "What's the problem?"

Dotty held up the bank's audit statement. "This is the problem." She spread the audit sheet on a long table. "I'm not an authority on these kinds of financial documents, but I think there something off about these calculations."

Mona looked down at the typed columns of numbers on the sheets. "What do you see?"

"If you ring up the numbers like I did, they come out all right, but look closely." Dotty handed Mona a magnifying glass. "Look at the sixes and nines."

Mona bent over and looked very carefully at the document. "Seems like the numbers have been switched. How's that possible?"

"A skilled typist can retrace a typewriter's strokes and remove the ink, then type over the space."

"Hmm. Did you calculate the numbers with the possible changes?"

"I did. Now, remember I am not a trained book accountant, but it looks like the Moon Bank is missing eighteen thousand dollars of deposits."

Mona was stunned and her knees felt a little weak. If Dotty was correct, this was very serious. "How could this have happened? We put in place every possible safeguard to protect our depositors."

"If there is a run on the bank, it will be discovered, and you will be charged with fraud since it is your bank."

Mona threw herself into a chair. "Dotty, can you fix me a gin and tonic please?" She thought again. "No. No. I need a clear head. Please order me a pot of hot tea and some light sandwiches. Order two cups. We are going over this audit sheet line by line."

Dotty rang the bell for Samuel while Mona hid their paperwork. The last thing Mona wanted was for the servants to discover that their life savings at her bank were in peril.

They sat silently next to each other in front of the fireplace until Samuel brought in the tray and they heard his footsteps recede down the corridor.

As Dotty was reaching for a sandwich, she said, "You know what you have to do."

Mona replied, "Yes, it's time I recall Rupert Hunt from Washington."

20

Wearing thick glasses and parting his hair down the middle with pomade, Rupert Hunt, applied for employment at the Moon Bank. He gave the bank manager several not-too-terribly enthusiastic letters of reference and basically fumbled through the interview. The manager, thinking Hunt an idiot, of course, gave Hunt the position of teller. This made the bank manager the number one suspect for embezzling the bank's assets in Hunt's eyes, for he should not have been hired by the Moon Bank or any other bank for that matter. It now came down to proving that Hunt was correct about the bank manager.

Hunt worked from nine in the morning until five every day. He got a half hour for lunch, which was spent across the street at the five and dime store's sandwich counter listening to the waitresses gossip. Once in a while he would treat himself to a strawberry malt—otherwise he would have the blue plate special with a cup of coffee. After work, he would follow the bank manager. For three days, Hunt trailed the bank manager home. The manager would stay there as per reports from Hunt's other operatives.

But something went awry on the fourth night. The bank manager went home, had his supper, and then went out again. Hunt's operative called him at the YMCA where he was boarding. "Boss, he went to a Rotary Club meeting for about fifteen minutes and then ducked out the back way."

"Where's he heading now?"

"He went to Belle Brezing's place."

"Interesting. Very interesting." Hunt lit a cigarette and used the light from his match to see if anyone was in the hallway. Hunt had to be careful as he was using the hall phone that everyone else used. "Stay put. If he comes out, follow him."

"Yes, boss."

"I'll be there in a few minutes. AND STAY

OUT OF SIGHT!" Hunt hung up the phone and ran back to his room, changing back into his good trousers and shirt. Within minutes he was completely dressed down to his hat, shoes, and dress suit. He would put most quick-change artists to shame. Walking calmly through the YMCA's lobby, Hunt then scurried out into the dark and up five blocks and then cut over to Megowan Street, where Brezing had her establishment on the east side of Lexington. Hunt motioned to his man, who watched from his car.

In most neighborhoods, people were sitting on their porches listening to their radio and enjoying the cool of the evening during the humid summers. Very few people sat outside their homes or took a stroll in this neighborhood. This was a bad section of town, and people tended to be more cautious. Hunt got in the car which was parked in the shadow thrown by a large magnolia tree.

Hunt asked, "Is he still in there?"

"He hasn't come out the front, but this is a two man job. He could have gone out the back way."

Brezing's place stood on a corner, but access

to see both the front and the back entrances was limited—too out in the open.

Hunt let it go, thinking he had made a mistake not putting two operatives on the job. He needed to get inside Brezing's house and see for himself. "Here goes," he said before opening the car door and walking across the street. He rang the doorbell and waited.

A maid dressed in a black uniform with a white apron opened the door. "Yes?"

"I would like to come in, please."

"Do you have an appointment, sir?"

"I understand you serve an excellent fare. I would like to partake."

The maid gave Hunt a queer look. "I'm sorry, sir, but Miss Brezing is retired and her establishment is closed to the public. Has been for many years."

"I've heard different."

"You've heard wrong. Good night, sir." The maid shut the sturdy wooden door quietly in Hunt's face.

Exasperated that he couldn't talk his way in, Hunt went over to the car. "Look, I'm going to the drug store to make a call. You stay here."

"Sure, boss."

Hunt walked back to Main Street, which was packed with people going to see a motion picture, getting an ice cream at the soda shop, or just window shopping for something to do in the evening. He went into the drug store and got in line, waiting for a customer to finish using the public telephone. Finally, it was his turn. Hunt fished a nickel from his vest pocket and hunching over so no one could read his lips, said into the phone, "Ver425."

After a few rings, someone answered. Hunt said, "I need Jellybean. Have him meet me in front of the cemetery." Receiving a reply, Hunt hung up and bought a pack of gum and a bottle of Coca-Cola before leaving. He drank the soda, but kept the glass bottle as a weapon. Both his personal and professional pride had been wounded tonight. He had messed up on the stakeout, and a maid had refused his entry into Brezing's place. It was the first time a bawdy house had refused him. It cut Hunt to the quick that such a place would rebuff him.

Hunt's cheeks burned at the thought of Mona Moon discovering that he could not get into a house of ill repute for reconnaissance. He had to make this right. Hunt had to have proof of who was in Belle's place without blowing his cover at the bank.

He just had to! It was a matter of honor with him.

21

The next day, Mona went to her bedroom to change as she was going boating with Robert on the Kentucky River. A bathing suit, lounging pants and canvas shoes were more in order. She was washing her face when she heard weeping coming from the maid's room where Violet slept. Concerned, she gently knocked on the connecting door. "Violet, may I come in, dear?"

"Yes. No. Yes. I guess okay."

Mona opened the door and saw Violet lying across her bed with cotton hankies, damp from tears, strewn about. Mona rushed over to her. "Violet, what's the matter? It can't be that bad, whatever it is."

Violet lifted her tear-stained face. "Oh, it is, Miss Mona. My life is over."

Mona chuckled and stroked Violet's hair. "You're so very young. You haven't even begun to live your life yet."

"Monty Putnam called and canceled his date with me."

Amused, Mona replied, "It's one date out of many in your life."

"He said his mother refused to let him go out with me because I worked for a harlot."

Mona drew back. "Oh, dear. I guess she was referring to me."

"I told him that I didn't care if I ever went out with him again because his breath stank like onions, and everyone knew his father ran off to live with a woman in Georgetown."

"I see. That was some telephone call."

"I *told* him," Violet said before blowing her nose and then discarding the handkerchief. She reached for a clean one.

"Yes, you did a good job of standing up for yourself. I'm proud of you."

"He called you something else."

"What was that?"

"A fornicator."

Mona took a deep breath. It made her angry

that men always attacked women's sexuality. "Well, I guess I am, strictly speaking."

"MISS MONA! You admit to such a thing?"

"Violet, I'm over twenty-one, in good health, financially stable, and know how to protect myself. If I want to be intimate with a man, it's nobody's business but mine."

"Does that go for me as well?"

"Absolutely not!" Mona was horrified.

Violet sat up in the bed and pouted. "Why are the rules different for me?"

Mona didn't really know why she felt that way, but she did. "You haven't finished your education, you're too young, and you need to have more life experience under your belt before taking such a step."

"Sounds kind of hypocritical if you ask me."

Mona laughed. "I guess it is. Now I know why hens hover over their chicks. Why all this sudden interest in the birds and the bees? Was Monty Putnam pressuring you?"

"He said he loved me and if I loved him, I should let him."

"Oh, Violet. That is one of the oldest tricks in the book. Please don't fall for nonsense like that.

Men are not in their right minds when it comes to sex. I can't explain it. Go ask your mother," Mona said, hoping to pass the buck.

"Does that go for Lord Farley?"

Mona did not correct Violet that the use of Lord was no longer the appropriate appellation for Robert. She kept the explanation of his new title for another day, although she felt most people would continue calling Robert—Lord Farley. "There are many men who would never even think of dishonoring a woman as it would impinge upon their principles. However, Lord Farley was young once and I know he was no saint, but he was very much in love with Lady Alice Morrell Nithercott. I have never asked whether they were intimate, and do not intend to. It's none of my business."

"What should I do?"

"Dry your tears and forget this Monty Putnam. He is not worth thinking about a second longer. There will be nicer men in your future, who will be worthy of your attention. I guarantee it. To put your mind at ease, have your young beaux meet me first. I'll make sure they understand rather quickly what will happen if they are not respectful."

Violet smiled. "Thank you, Miss Mona. I feel better."

"Tell me one thing. Does Mr. Putnam go to your church?"

"Yes, he does."

"Is he an associate of Jacob Gentry?"

"Mr. Gentry is his Sunday school teacher."

"I see." It was obvious to Mona that Jacob Gentry was trying to ruin her reputation alongside her associates by sexual innuendo. Had he put Monty Putnam up to deflower Violet? Mona thought the answer was yes—the filthy bugger. She lived in a very conservative, religious community where men used sex as a weapon against women. Mona had to be careful. "If I were you, Violet, I would think about switching churches."

Violet's eyes widened. "You think I was a target?"

"I would like to err on the side of caution. I'm very sorry that you might be swept up in my battles, but that's just the way it is."

"Oh, I'm so mad. Why didn't I see that? Violet blushed. "Why wasn't I angry when Monty suggested getting between the sheets? I should have slapped his face and called his mother."

Mona put her arms around Violet and gave a quick hug. "You didn't because you were flattered at the attention. Because you had never been in a situation like that before and were inexperienced in handling it. Because you're young—so very young. Don't be hard on yourself. It happens to every young lady."

"Even you, Miss Mona?"

"When I was in college, I met a nice young man who courted me. I thought I was in love. I thought we were in love. Things turned upside down when he started pressuring me to go to bed with him. I was very confused. If he loved me, why would he risk me getting pregnant? If I was with child and unmarried, I would be forced to leave the university in disgrace and my future would be over. It was then I realized there is a difference between lust and love. Remember that, Violet. Don't throw your future away over a man. Always carve out your own path."

"When did you decide that Lord Farley was Mr. Right?"

"We're not one of those lovey-dovey couples like Mr. and Mrs. Deatherage, but I knew something was afoot when I realized that I ached for

Robert when he was not about. I'm not talking about the physical aspect of our relationship. I'm referring to something deeper. I don't feel complete when he's not with me. I crave to see him, smell him, hear his voice. His very presence gives me comfort." Mona lifted Violet's chin. "But as much as I love Robert, I will not take him as a drinking man. I have never loved unconditionally and I never will. If he doesn't keep his promise not to drink, I will leave him."

"Oh, no, Miss Mona. That would kill Lord Farley."

"I know. It would kill me also, but I'd rather give Robert up so I wouldn't have to face being disappointed or even hate him over a bottle of whiskey. If that happened, I think the better part of me would die. I would rather leave him with our memories and love intact."

"I'm never going to accept a date again. It's all too much."

"Love is a minefield, for sure, Violet, but you will find devotion from a man and have a happy life. I just feel it." Mona kissed Violet on the forehead. "No more tears, sweet girl. You are too pretty, the day is too beautiful, and good fortune is just around the corner. Fix your face and go visit your mother. You'll be in the pink again before you know it."

"Thank you, Miss Mona, but I'd rather not visit my mother. I don't want her to know about this just yet. It's so embarrassing. I can't believe that I even contemplated such a thing."

"Your mother won't hear a thing from me, I promise, but I think you should tell her what Putnum suggested." Mona looked at her watch. "Goodness. Look at the time. I'm late."

"I'll be fine, Miss Mona. You don't want to keep Lord Farley waiting."

"Well, then get along with you. The day is wasting."

Violet grinned. "Yes, Miss Mona. I will."

Mona hurried into her spacious and luxurious green tiled bathroom and changed into her swimming attire—bathing suit, pants, and top to protect her delicate pale skin, and floppy hat. Mona turned to her white poodle who was watching from the master bed. "Come on, Chloe. Want to take a trip on the river?"

Excited, Chloe wagged her tail and jumped down. She happily followed Mona through the kitchen, where Samuel put a picnic basket and flasks of lemonade, water, and sweet iced tea into a farm pickup. After telling Samuel that she should be back in three hours, Mona put Chloe in the truck and started the vehicle, making her way to the back of the Moon property where several boats were docked on the river.

Mona parked under the shade of a sycamore tree, and she and Chloe got out. Chloe ran to the river and jumped in. Mona walked about and then checked the boats.

Robert was not there. That was odd. He was usually on time. It was she who was late. Mona waited another half hour, but Robert didn't show. Concerned, she gathered a wet Chloe and drove to Robert's house, but it was locked and his car was gone. Mona let herself in with a key Robert had hidden under a rock in his garden. The house was quiet and dark, even on such a sunny day. "Robert! Robert! Are you here?" Mona waited for an answer and hearing none, she searched each room in the house. He was not home, and nothing had been disturbed. Mona had a sinking feeling. It was not like Robert to miss an assignation.

Mona went back to Moon Manor, ignoring the surprised looks of her staff. From the library, she made a call to Dexter after making sure no servants were lurking in the hallway. "Hello, Dexter. This is Mona. Is Robert with you?" She listened to Dexter. "He's not. I see. Listen to me. Robert didn't show up for an outing with me. I've been to his home. He's not there and his car is gone. It's not like him to forget a rendezvous. We were to go boating." She listened on the phone. "Yes, that would be good to look for him in town, but be very discreet. I don't want this made into an incident for the papers. It could be as innocent as a flat tire. Let me know when you find something out. Yes. Thanks. Goodbye."

After placing the receiver back in its cradle, Mona went upstairs to change into a day frock. The afternoon came and went. At eight o'clock, she dressed formally for dinner and ate alone in the dining room. Afterward, Mona had coffee in the drawing room and read the papers while listening for the phone. Every time she heard a noise that sounded like a car door closing, she ran to the windows. Finally, exhausted and worried, Mona climbed the grand marble staircase to her bedroom.

Something was wrong, and it was all Mona could do not to burst into tears. She dreaded the new day to come and the terrible news it might bring.

Where was Lawrence Robert Emerton Dagobert Farley, the Duke of Brynelleth?

22

Aroused from a fitful sleep, Mona heard Chloe growl from the bedroom balcony. She jumped out of bed and found her poodle reared up on the balcony's balustrade. "What is it, girl? What do you hear?" Mona followed Chloe's gaze and saw lights flickering through the trees. Someone was in Robert's house!

Mona threw a coat over her black negligee and slipped into some boots. Gathering a flashlight and her gun, she flew down the staircase and out the front door, not even bothering to close it. Hurrying down the well-worn path between Moon Manor and Robert's house, Mona stopped at the edge of the tree line. There were three cars in the driveway—Robert's, Dexter's, and a Moon vehicle the Pinkertons used. Hmm.

She crept around the house, looking in the windows until she found the four men in the kitchen. Mona watched Dexter coaxing a disheveled Robert to drink coffee.

Chloe barked excitedly.

"Hush, girl," Mona admonished.

It was too late. Dexter heard the dog barking and stepped out the kitchen door. "Who's there?"

Mona moved into the light coming from the kitchen window. "What's going on, Dexter?"

Dexter looked rumpled wearing no tie and his shirt buttons undone to mid-chest. His tousled hair emphasized his puffy eyes red from the lack of sleep. "Go home, Mona. I'll take care of this."

"The hell I will," Mona said as she and Chloe brushed past Dexter. She found Robert slumped over the kitchen table, snoring, and reeking of booze. Shocked, Mona asked the Pinkertons, "Where did you find him?"

They looked at each other and then glanced at Dexter, who was standing behind Mona with his arms akimbo.

"Don't look at Mr. Deatherage. He's not your boss. I am. Where did you find His Grace?"

One of the Pinkertons reluctantly said, "We

found him like this in his car parked at Belle
Brezing's house."

Dexter explained, "Mona, sometimes men
slip. That doesn't mean they don't love their
women. It just means there was a momentary
weakness. Don't judge Robert too harshly."

"I'm not judging Robert at all. If you took
time to notice, Robert's been rousted. There is a
bruise forming on his cheek and there are cuts on
his lips. His knuckles are damaged as though he
scuffled with someone. He reeks of whiskey as if
someone doused him with it."

Mona leaned over and sniffed Robert's head.
"It's even in his hair. Robert is a tidy drinker. No.
No. Robert was attacked and they forced liquor
on him. This was a classic setup to make Robert
look like a drunk."

"I'm afraid there is more bad news."

"Let me guess. The papers got a photograph
of Robert in his car at Belle's house."

"I'm afraid so."

"What a coincidence. The papers just happen
to show up when Robert was parked outside
Belle's."

"How are we going to put a spin on this?"

"I'm tired of playing defensively. It's time to get ugly. Call the papers and threaten, wheedle, or bribe them not to run a story on this. Then call Sheriff Monahan and report that Robert has been assaulted. Take pictures of his injuries tomorrow morning. Get someone over to Belle's house tonight and get statements. Someone arranged this little tableau, and I'm going to make them pay." She turned to the Pinkertons. "Get His Grace into the shower and put him to bed. Leave his clothes on the kitchen table. We might need them as evidence. Stay with him until he wakes up and is coherent. Then report back to Moon Manor."

"Yes, Miss Moon," the Pinkertons said in unison.

Dexter warned, "Mona, you're playing a dangerous game here. We don't know who is behind this."

"I've been warned that Jacob Gentry is spreading rumors about me around town. I have a strong suspicion that dear Aunt Melanie is in cahoots with Jacob Gentry and stirring him up. Well, I'm going to strike back."

"If you insist, but I caution you against it."

Mona grinned, "Dexter, you know that saying—hell hath no fury like a woman scorned? Well, hell hath no fury like Mona Moon angry."

Dexter whistled. "I'm beginning to see that is true. I pity the poor blighter who is caught up in this."

Mona caressed Robert's dirty and matted hair. "So do I, Dexter. So do I."

23

Dexter called Mona late the next morning to tell her the papers wouldn't print the story, and the negatives of the pictures they took were already in Dexter's hands. Mona told him to hold onto them as they might be needed later on. When she asked who tipped the papers, Dexter replied they said it was an unidentified caller.

"How convenient," Mona said, sarcastically. "How is Robert doing? I want to see him."

"Don't, Mona. He wouldn't want you to see him in this condition. It's not dignified."

Mona didn't reply to Dexter's suggestion as she understood how proud Robert was. Instead, she asked, "Has the incident been reported to the authorities?"

"We went to see Sheriff Monahan this morning first thing. It was awfully rough on Robert, but he insisted. Now the papers can run with the story, giving Robert's attack a more truthful slant rather than raw sensationalism."

"Where's Robert now?"

"We went to my doctor and after his examination, I drove Robert home to recuperate." Dexter advised again, "Give him a few days, Mona. He needs to catch his breath. He was pummeled pretty good."

"I'll stay away," Mona promised, realizing Robert had made this request. "Keep me posted." Hanging the phone up, Mona leaned back in her chair, relieved. They had skirted one disaster. Now it was time for Mona to take action with another problem—her Aunt Melanie. Gathering four Pinkertons, Violet, Samuel, and Jamison, Mona drove to Melanie's house and barged in. After all, she owned it. "Aunt Melanie! Melanie!"

Melanie angrily strutted from the garden where she was having a luncheon with her friends. "What is all this caterwauling?" She stopped short when she spied Mona and her entourage. "Mona, what in the blazes are you doing here? Where is Violet going?" Melanie shouted at Violet, who was climbing the stairs to the second floor. "Come down, girl. You have no business up there."

Mona grabbed Melanie's arm and dragged her into the morning room, shutting the door. The two women angrily faced each other. It was ironic they looked so similar to each other. Both were comparable in height and weight, and they had the same coloring, though Melanie's hair was a shade darker—a light blond instead of platinum. They could almost be taken for sisters, but they were worlds apart in temperament.

If Melanie knew the source of Mona's annoyance, she showed no sign of it. She shook herself free from Mona. "Get off. You're embarrassing me in front of my friends."

"I'm going to do more than that, Melanie. Violet is upstairs packing your steamer trunks. You are going on an extended cruise to South America, and you're going to stay there until I say you can come back."

"You must be insane," Melanie hissed. "I'm not going anywhere."

"If you don't leave this afternoon, I am going to have you thrown out of this house."

Melanie gasped, "You can't. We have an agreement. I have a contract that you signed."

"And that contract says if you work to undermine my position, it is null and void."

Melanie flung herself in a chair, looking smug. "I don't know what you are talking about."

"I know that you are working with Jacob Gentry to discredit me and ruin my reputation."

"You have no proof."

"So you don't deny it."

"I don't need to deny anything. You need to prove it. In a court of law."

"Very few people know about Robert's problem with alcohol. You are one of them."

"Lots of men have problems with drink or laudanum or cocaine. Most men I know who fought in the Great War are addicted to something. Alcohol just happens to be Robert's vice of choice."

"But the only person who would use that knowledge against Robert is you."

"Did something untoward happen?" Melanie asked innocently, reaching for a cigarette box on a table.

Mona marched over to Melanie and knocked

the box out of her hand. "You ever harm Robert again, I'll kill you, Melanie. I really will, so you better get on that ship for your own sake. It's all I can do not to pull my gun out and shoot you right now."

Melanie's eyes widened with fear, but she bravely argued, "Murder me with all these witnesses in my back yard? I think not."

"Oh, I wouldn't do it now. I'd wait until you were alone. I have no intention of going to jail over you. As soon as Violet has packed your things, Samuel will put your trunks in the car and four Pinkertons will escort you to the railway station. You will catch a connection to Miami and from there a boat to Havana. The cruise will end in Rio de Janerio. I have reserved a suite for you there. Here are the tickets." Mona threw a packet of documents, schedules, reservations, visas, and money into Melanie's lap. "Say goodbye to your guests and change into your traveling clothes. You're leaving within the hour."

"What excuse shall I use?"

"I don't give an owl's hoot what you say, just get out of town." Mona turned and left a stunned Melanie sitting cockeyed in a chintz chair.

As soon as Mona left, Melanie tore open the packet and counted the money. It was over ten thousand dollars. She thought for a moment and considered the ocean cruise. Rich men were always on these types of voyages. Maybe she could snag a rich husband. Maybe Mona was doing her a favor. With the money, she could live like a queen in South America for quite some time.

Thinking this might be her ticket to get out from under Mona's thumb, Melanie ran for her bedroom to help Violet pack her things.

24

Four days later, Mona was having breakfast in the garden when Robert sat down and poured himself a cup of coffee. Acting nonchalantly, Mona slid over a glazed donut. "Here, I know how much you like to dunk donuts in your coffee."

She rang a bell.

Samuel came out. "Yes, miss?"

"Please scramble some eggs for His Grace."

"Sunny-side, Samuel," Robert interjected. "And a tall glass of orange juice, please."

"Yes, sir. Coming right up."

Mona and Robert watched Samuel leave the garden.

As soon as he was out of sight, Mona asked, "How do you feel?"

"Like a mule kicked me. It was decent of you to hire a nurse."

"I thought you needed a few days to recuperate. I'm glad Dexter insisted that you return home after reporting the incident to the sheriff and get some rest. You needed a good sleep-in." Mona grinned. "By the way, that's a nice shiner you've got there."

Robert returned the grin. "Yes, it's turning to the yellow and purple phase now. I would like to say I gave as well as I got, but that would be a lie. What do you Southerners say—I got my ass whooped."

"I wouldn't know. I'm from New York."

Robert chuckled and then winced. "Ouch, it even hurts to laugh."

"Why did you and Dexter go see Sheriff Monahan rather than have him come to you?"

"I wanted the good sheriff's staff to see my injuries. I didn't want to give Monahan an out saying they weren't severe and play down my attack."

"Oh, you don't trust our good lawman?"

"I don't trust anyone."

"Does that include me?"

Robert looked pained. "If there is one person on earth I do trust, it would be you."

Mona looked pleased and reached out her hand to Robert.

He took it and squeezed. "Mona, I have to ask. Are we finished?"

"What do you mean, darling?"

"Are we done? No longer engaged?"

Mona shook her head. "Where did you get that crazy idea?"

"I know how you feel about my drinking."

Mona was aghast. "You must think me a heartless creature if you could imagine I would abandon you in such a time of crisis. I know you didn't drink of your own volition. I'm ready to listen if you wish to tell the story."

"You mean the papers didn't do a story?"

"The papers did a nice small piece on your attack. I saved the clippings for your scrapbook," Mona teased. On a more serious note, she said, "Made you look very sympathetic, but I'd like to hear what happened from you."

Interrupting their conversation, Samuel laid down a plate of sunny-side up eggs with bacon in front of Robert. He also placed a large glass of a dark-looking liquid beside his plate.

"What is this?" Robert asked, looking up at Samuel.

"Mr. Thomas said to drink it. It's hair of the dog that bit you."

Robert pushed it away, embarrassed that Mona's servants knew of his beating. Of course, how could he deny it as his face was still covered in cuts and bruises? "I'm over the hangover stage now. That incident was days ago, and I can't have any pick-me-ups with alcohol in it." Robert sniffed the glass. "Besides, it smells nasty."

'Yes, sir, it does stink, but it will take away your blues and get you moving. Don't worry. Mr. Thomas didn't put any alcohol in it. You've been sleeping for days now. Mr. Thomas says you need to get in the sunshine and get your mind on other things."

Mona laughed. "You better do it, Robert. Mr. Thomas commands it."

"Tell Mr. Thomas thank you. I will certainly drink it."

Samuel nodded and left.

Robert mugged at Mona. "Mr. Thomas cares. What do you know." He took a sip of the drink.

"Oh, gosh, that's awful." He handed it to Mona.

Mona took a sip. "Tomato juice, Worcestershire sauce, pepper, lemon juice, and a raw egg." She handed the glass back to Robert. "You better drink it. You know they are watching from the upstairs window."

"Including Mr. Thomas?"

Mona laughed. "The kitchen staff, but they will report to Mr. Thomas. All of my staff would make great spies."

Robert held his side while joining in the laughter.

"Ribs still tender?" Mona asked, concerned.

"I'll be all right. Don't worry."

"Can you tell me what happened?"

"To tell you the truth, I don't remember much. I was at the racecourse looking at a horse I was interested in. I told the owner I would get back to him. I needed to think the purchase over as I thought he was asking too much for the animal. I was heading back to my car when three men jumped me and pulled me into an empty horse stall."

"Do you remember what they looked like?"

"Two of them. I gave a description to the

sheriff. As for the third one, I only heard his voice. He said, 'Don't beat him up too badly, boys. We don't want to kill him.' The next thing I knew your men found me folded up in my car next to Belle's. I remember Dexter speaking to me." Robert shook his head. "Very little after that. It's all a blur."

"Oh, Robert, I'm so sorry. I feel as though I am to blame. There's much I need to discuss with you. I haven't because I've been so pressed for time and so very tired." Mona looked down at her hands, ashamed of herself. "I was so angry with your solicitors, but I realized they were just a distraction. The real problem was close to home. A viper was let loose because I took my eyes off her. I should have known better."

"I don't know what you mean, Mona."

"I've sent Melanie packing. She's on her way to Rio."

"Bravo, Mona, but what brought this about?"

"I think Melanie is behind a lot of my recent trouble."

"What trouble? What has happened?"

Mona took a deep breath and said, "Robert, there is money missing from the bank. If I don't recover those deposits, I could go to jail for fraud."

Robert looked shocked. This was serious business. "How could Melanie cause money to be missing?"

"I don't know. I just believe that if Melanie is not around, things will go smoother."

"But, darling, if you think your aunt has something to do with the embezzlement, why let her go?"

"To protect the Moon name. I've got to find that money and catch the thief before the bank is audited by the banking commission."

"No wonder you have been out of sorts. And to think you had to deal with my knuckled-headed solicitors on top of that. I'm so sorry, my dear."

"Robert, I think all the mischief that has been happening lately is connected. I don't think they are isolated incidents."

"You mean you think there has been an orchestrated campaign against us?"

"Not so much us—me. It's to run me out of town, and they are pitting us against each other."

"I think you're getting paranoid, Mona."

"Not really. There's the bank's missing money, the missing Hancock Jeter, missing Moon patents, the murder at Belle's, Violet's incident with her beau, and your beating."

"Violet had an incident?"

"Stay focused, Robert. You must remember that Melanie is considered a real Moon. She has many loyal supporters in the community. I am a usurper who took Melanie's rightful place as head of Moon Enterprises. My father was disowned by the Moon family for marrying the gardener's daughter. They think Uncle Manfred was crazy to leave me Moon Manor and the mining business. And there are those who disdain me because they don't like my progressive views."

"Like pay equality for all of your employees and having a bank that caters to women customers?"

"Exactly. The fact that my bank will not let husbands have access to their wives' accounts has angered a great many men in our community. Of course, the bank would be a target."

"Well, we have some options here."

"Such as?"

"We get married as soon as possible and go

live at Brynelleth, leaving this mess behind us."

Mona frowned. "Not going to happen."

Robert smirked. "I didn't think so." He turned more serious. "You tell me what to do, Mona, and I'll do it. I'm at your disposal."

Mona started to say something when she spied Dotty walking toward them. "Hush. We'll talk about this later."

"I'm sorry to interrupt the two of you, but I think you need to know about this immediately, Mona," Dotty said.

Robert jumped up and pulled out a chair for the secretary. "You look ashen, Dotty. Please sit down."

"Thank you. In fact, we should all be sitting down."

"Let me have the bad news," Mona said, bracing herself. She felt butterflies flutter in her stomach.

"Mr. Deatherage just called. Someone has filed a complaint again Moon Bank, and it is going to be audited."

Mona glanced at Robert. "See, I told you."

He nodded in concurrence.

"Is that all?" Mona asked.

Dotty looked surprised. "Isn't that enough?"

Robert asked, "Do we know who filed the complaint and what the specifics are?"

"Not at the moment, but Mr. Deatherage is looking into the matter. He'll phone when he finds something out."

"I think it's time I start to act on the offensive or this is going to railroad me into jail." She turned to Dotty. "Let's start with you."

"Me?" Dotty asked, looking back and forth between Mona and Robert.

"Are you still seeing Jacob Gentry's assistant?"

Dotty looked surprised. "I am, but I can assure you that no information has passed from me to him."

"Are you fond of him?"

"I think we are getting serious."

"Does he visit you at your cottage on the Moon estate?"

"He picks me up for our dates and brings me home."

"Does he go inside your home?"

"I've invited him in for coffee and a slice of pie, but he never stays more than an hour. We're not doing anything that would embarrass you, Mona."

"You keep a desk at your cottage with Moon documents."

"I sometimes take work home."

Gowing uneasy, Dotty asked, "What are you getting at?"

"I'm getting at that you are dating a man who works for a man who publicly despises me. I think that is a grave conflict of interest."

Dotty squinted her eyes. "I would never betray your trust. What are you planning to do?"

Mona looked squarely at Dotty. "Just this. You're fired!"

25

Mona waited as she heard Samuel open the front door and usher Dotty into the library.

Dotty threw her hat and gloves into a chair. She sadly shook her head at Mona while taking a chair across from her. "You have a fire lit on such a warm night."

"I know, but the fire is cheerful. Is the room too warm?"

"No, I feel a chill."

"I take it that the date with your beau didn't go well. I apologize for putting you through this ordeal, but I strongly felt that he was using your position to wheedle information for his boss, Jacob Gentry. I needed to know for sure, which is why I devised this little subterfuge of firing you."

"It went as you said it would. You were right."

Mona could see the pain in Dotty's face and she felt terrible about putting her through this ordeal. "Isn't better to know now rather than later when you've invested more time and emotions?"

"I guess." Dotty poured herself a cup of tea from the tea service laid on the table next to her chair. She looked around. "Got anything stronger than this?"

Ignoring Dotty's request for liquor, Mona said, "I'm sorry about how things turned out."

"Don't worry about me, Mona. I'll get over this. It's just that I really liked him and feel the fool for falling for his act."

"Tell me what happened."

"I see now how he was pumping me for information. He asked about my day, where I had been—general questions one asks a close friend in casual conversation. I had skirted these questions before, but thought them innocuous. They weren't." Dotty took a sip of tea before relating the rest of her story. "We went to dinner and afterwards strolled down Main Street, looking in the display windows. I played it just the way you said to. He asked what the matter was. I told him that you had fired me, and I needed to move off the Moon property by the end of the week. I asked if he would help me move my things into town, relating that I was going to stay at the hotel until I found a new job and permanent lodging."

Mona leaned forward in her chair and placed her hand on Dotty's arm. "Then what happened?"

"He seemed genuinely concerned for my well-being, made sympathetic noises, and then asked if I still had access to Moon Enterprise's files. I told him that all my keys had been confiscated, and I was barred from Moon Manor and Moon Enterprises. Suddenly, he said he needed to leave as he had to get up early for work. When I asked if he was going to help me move, he said he would call. He gave me a brisk kiss on the cheek and left me standing without an escort or transportation home. I had to call Jamison from the drugstore to come and get me."

Both women sat in silence.

"I'm truly sorry," Mona finally said. "No one likes to be used, but in this job, I'm afraid it will happen again. If you wish to resign, I understand."

"No. No. I'll stay," Dotty said wearily. "You warned me about dating Jacob Gentry's employee. Besides, where else can I get a job that pays so well? This is just a small bump in the road of life, I guess."

"That's not good enough, Dotty. I can refer you for jobs in other companies that have similar pay. Money is not an issue. I need to have people near me that are loyal and believe in the principles that I do. Think it over. If you wish to leave my employment, I can give you a very reasonable severance package."

"That's good of you to do so, but I'd rather not discuss it right now. I feel battered and would like to go home."

"Of course. We'll discuss this another time." Mona stood. "I'll have one of the Pinkertons escort you to your cottage. It's dark and the moon is not out."

"Thank you." Dotty gave Mona a hard look. "You know, I can't help but hate you a little right now."

"You need to direct that anger toward Jacob

Gentry and your young man. Women don't have the luxury of living in a fool's paradise."

"I hope someday to return the favor, Mona."

Taking Dotty's words as a threat, Mona stood. "You need to go home and sleep this off. We can talk about it later."

"You're right. I'm not thinking straight."

Mona walked Dotty to the front veranda and motioned to a Pinkerton guarding the front of the house. "Good night, Dotty."

"Bonne nuit, Mona."

Mona watched a despondent Dotty and the guard walk in the direction of her cottage, knowing that Dotty wished her anything but a good night.

26

It was after eleven at night when the bank manager quietly let himself into the Moon Bank building through the back door. Using a flashlight, he stealthily made his way to the large walk-in vault that required a key and a number combination. He rotated the safe's combination and opened the heavy metal door, which led to another gateway that was reminiscent of a jail cell door. Using the bank's master key, he unlocked a barred steel metal door to allow final entry into the safe where cash and deposit boxes were located.

Gleefully, he pocketed a thousand in fives and relocked the vault's two doors. Going into his office, the manager rearranged figures that were penciled in the bank's official ledger. Tomorrow his secretary would type the report for Mona Moon and other bank officials, never knowing she was typing false information. The bank manager had been skimming money for the past six months, and no one had noticed the discrepancies. He felt he was a very clever man, indeed. He was on his way out when lights came on in the bank. Confused, he froze, looking about.

"Over here, bub," he heard a voice say.

The bank manager blinked in the strong light and saw a man lazily leaning against the loan officer's desk. He blinked again in the strong light. "Mr. Hunt?"

"That's right."

"What are you doing here at this time of night?" The bank manager said, wondering if he could pin the robbery on Hunt.

"Catching little weasels like yourself. Oh, by the way, all the entrances are guarded by Pinkerton men. I wouldn't make a run for it, if I were you. They all have blackjacks and are just itching to use them."

"I don't know what you mean. I had forgotten my briefcase. Why are you here and how do you have a key to the bank?"

Rupert Hunt twirled a key ring around his index finger. "But I do." He went over to the bank manager and shoved him into a chair.

Blustering, the bank manager jumped up and pushed Hunt out of the way, running for the back door. Wrenching it open, he found three Pinkertons guarding the entrance. He turned with his eyes wide with fright, his jaw dropping wide in astonishment.

"I told you so," Hunt said. "Now you come back and sit down like a good boy. There is someone who wants to talk with you."

Hunter led the dazed bank manager back into the main lobby when the front entrance opened and Mona Moon walked in. Behind her followed Dexter Deatherage.

The manager moaned when he saw Mona looking very disapprovingly at him. She motioned for him to sit in the applicant's chair across from the loan desk. She sat behind the desk while Deatherage stood.

"Well, Mr. Bludger, it seems you have been a busy boy with my customer's money."

"I can explain."

"I'm sure you can and you are going to."

Deatherage handed Mona several important-looking documents. She laid them on the top of the desk. "You have some decisions to make in the next few moments. First—you are going to tell us if you worked alone or in cahoots with someone else. Second—where's the money?"

"I don't know what you're talking about. I just came to get my briefcase."

Mona looked disappointed and motioned to Hunt to search Mr. Bludger, who protested vigorously, slapping Hunt's hands away.

"Stop it, pal. I'm dyin' to belt you one," Hunt warned, holding a blackjack.

Mr. Bludger looked beseechingly at Mona, who nodded at Hunt.

"He will, Mr. Bludger. Mr. Hunt is not a very nice man. That's precisely why I hired him."

"Miss Moon, I must object to this behavior. It is very unladylike."

"I never said I was a lady. What I am is a bank owner who *objects* to my employees stealing from the bank." Mona stood and walked around the desk and sat on the edge. "This is what is going to happen to you, my good man. If you don't give us the information we need, I am going to call the good Sheriff Monahan, who will place you in handcuffs. The arrest will be in the afternoon papers. Your wife and children will be ashamed and probably shunned by the community. They will have to leave town. Your wife will divorce you when you are convicted and sent to jail. Meanwhile, the Moon Bank will be audited and shut down. Employees will lose their jobs and they will hate you as well."

"Oh no," wailed Mr. Bludger, who threw his hands up in despair. "NO! NO! My family is everything to me."

"The alternative is that you make a complete confession, tell us where the money is, and sign the various documents in front of you. Once that is done, you will announce your new position as a manager at the Moon copper mine in Butte, Montana."

"Montana?" Mr. Bludger gulped, tugging at his collar.

"We will relocate you and your family out west."

"I know nothing about mining."

"That doesn't matter because you won't last. Two months after working at the mine office, you will tell your wife that you don't like Montana and wish to relocate again. I hear southern California is nice."

"What?"

"You will leave our employment, and we hope to never hear from you again. It's that or jail, but either way you will leave this area and this state, never to step foot in Kentucky again or have anything to do with Moon Enterprises once you leave our employment permanently in a few months."

"Take the deal, man. Don't be a fool," Hunt encouraged. "You've been caught red-handed."

Dexter added, "The sentence for embezzling from a bank can be twenty years."

Tears dripped down Mr. Bludger's face. Seeing that he was defeated, he reached into his pocket and pulled out the wad of five dollar bills.

"Why Mr. Bludger?" Mona asked, taking the money from him.

"You're upsetting the apple cart, Miss Moon. You come down here from the North with your new fangled ideas and try to tell us that how we live is wrong. We have a wonderful culture and tradition that many of us are trying to preserve.

We aim to make an example out of you."

"What you say is true, Mr. Bludger. I have money and power, which I will use to further my agenda. I believe that women should have control over their own money. Many of our depositors put two or five dollars into their accounts every week. They work as waitresses, cooks, teachers, seamstresses. If we didn't protect their money, their husbands or fathers would take advantage and withdraw their funds. What angers me is that banks let men, who have abandoned their homes, still have access to their wives' money. These men drain their wives' savings and then run off to ride the rails and live as a hobo. Now you may think it is okay for a man to take his wife's money without her permission, but I don't. I want this bank to guard women's interests."

Bludger protested, "Woman is the handmaiden of man."

Mona rolled her eyes. "You were supposed to protect these accounts, Mr. Bludger, just as you were supposed to protect all the farmers' accounts as well. It was your duty."

"My duty was to obey God's word."

'No, my dear Mr. Bludger. Your duty was not

to steal from those whom you were supposed to shield. I despise men like you, who make the job of living so difficult for others."

"Enough of the philosophical debate," Dexter interjected. "Mr. Bludger, the cards are on the table. Either tell us all you know or we will ruin you. It's that simple. You've played the game and have lost. What's it going to be?"

"I'll cooperate," Mr. Bludger whispered. "I know when I'm beaten."

"Good. How much money has been embezzled?"

"About twenty thousand including two thousand I took for my own use."

Dexter sat behind the desk and Mona pulled up a chair beside Dexter.

"Was anyone working with you who is employed at the bank?"

Bludger wiped his face with his handkerchief. "No."

"You worked alone?"

"I mean no one else at the bank was involved."

Dexter furiously wrote on a legal pad. "Who else was involved?"

Bludger hesitated and then said, "No one."

Hunt slapped the fedora hat off Mr. Bludger's head. "Come on, now. You're lying."

Mona spoke up. "Thank you, Mr. Hunt, but that is quite enough."

"It's your funeral."

Mona gave Hunt a stern look. "You must give a complete confession or no deal."

"I don't know everyone but I got my orders from Jacob Gentry."

Mona asked, "Orders? You are not an equal partner, but a soldier."

"Jacob wants to run for governor on abolishing votes by women. He wants the 19th amendment in Kentucky overturned. I gave the money to him to fund his future campaign."

Dexter asked, "Do you know where he keeps it?"

Bludger shook his head. "I have no idea."

"How did you think the amendment was going to be overturned?"

"If Gentry got voted in, he could persuade the Kentucky legislature that it was their duty as Christian men to overturn women's voting rights."

Dexter turned to Mona. "There are other states fighting the same fight, and most states in the South have not ratified the 19th amendment."

Mona could hardly hide her contempt. "In addition to stealing, your little cabal tried to compromise my employees, Miss Violet and Miss Dotty."

"They are Jezebels just like you are," Bludger sneered.

Mona reached over and slapped Bludger's face. "How dare you denigrate such lovely women who are worth ten of you! You and your merry men make me sick."

"Mona, control yourself," admonished Dexter. "I'll handle this."

Hunt laughed. "Atta girl." He leaned over in Bludger's face. "That's why I work for Mona Moon. You always know where you stand with her—and the fact she pays me a great deal of money."

Irritated, Dexter asked, "Please let me handle this, both of you. All these threats of violence are unnecessary."

"Very well," Mona said.

Dexter asked, "Where is Hancock Jeter?"

Bludger's eyes widened. "I don't know."

"But he is part of your group?"

Bludger remained quiet.

"Mr. Bludger, shall I remind you what will happen if you don't cooperate?"

Hunt said, "All these men go to the same church. Yeah, Jeter was part of this."

"Was he the only one, Mr. Bludger?" Dexter asked.

"We have men everywhere in Moon Enterprises. This is just the beginning to bring you down, Mona Moon."

"Was Jeter ordered to steal the drilling patent?"

"Yes, Mr. Deatherage, he was and the patent has already been sold to a rival mining company."

"Where is Mr. Jeter?" Dexter asked again.

"I don't know. Really, I don't. He has kinfolk in Cynthiana."

"Give me the list of names of men who have infiltrated Moon Enterprises."

Bludger reluctantly gave six names.

Mona asked, "Who is Mira Hedge?"

Bludger looked bewildered. "How should I know?"

"You've never heard of a Mira Hedge?"

"She's one of Belle's girls. I've never had any contact with her. Look, I've told you all I know."

"We shall see. The Pinkertons will drive you to Cincinnati where you will catch the early morning train out west. Several of our men will accompany you."

Bludger gasped. "I can't even pack a bag or say goodbye to my family?"

"Once we conclude that what you have told us is true, we will send your family to you. I will personally see your wife early in the morning to tell her that you had to leave on bank business. She'll believe me."

Dexter nodded to the Pinkertons standing nearby. They marched up to Mr. Bludger and each took hold of him under the arms. Mr. Bludger protested vigorously, but to no avail.

Mona watched them leave the bank through the back door and waited to hear several car doors slam shut and motors rev up. She turned to Dexter. "One down and more to go."

"Mona, we have a serious security issue here," Dexter said. "We thought with good wages and working conditions we'd be safe from strikes and internal company strife. We are going to have to spend a great deal of time routing out this nest of provocateurs."

"Why don't we start by cutting off the head of the main snake? I think if we do that, the rest might slink back into the shadows."

"I'm game, if you are. We need to strike fast before it is known that Bludger has left town."

Mona smiled. "I know where the main viper is this very moment. Let's pay him a call. Shall we, gentlemen?"

Dexter, Mona, and Hunt all grinned at each other. They knew exactly where they were going next.

27

Mona knocked on the front door of Belle Brezing's establishment.

A maid opened and was startled to see Mona standing on the porch stoop alone after midnight. "I'm sorry, miss, but women are not allowed in without an escort after the sun sets."

"You must remember me from several weeks ago. I am here to see Miss Brezing."

"Sorry, Miss Moon, but Miss Brezing is entertaining other guests at the moment."

"Precisely," Mona said, pushing her way past the maid.

Pinkertons rushed in after her and ran up the stairs, bursting into all the bedrooms while more Pinkertons hustled in the back way with cameras, taking pictures of everyone.

Mona strolled into the parlor where four men and Belle Brezing had been playing cards. Jacob Gentry, including several other men, stood in astonishment while Belle calmly asked for an explanation. "What's the meaning of this, Miss Moon?"

"It's a raid of sorts, Miss Belle. It seems that Mr. Gentry here has been planning my demise using your establishment as headquarters. I hardly believe that you knew nothing about it."

Nonplussed, Brezing asked, "What do you plan to do?"

One of the Pinkertons took several photographs of Jacob Gentry and his cohorts with Belle Brezing.

"Grab him!" screamed an enraged Gentry as he lunged for the Pinkerton.

Rupert Hunt, rushing in behind the Pinkerton, pulled out a pistol and shot into the floor. "Stay where you are. There is no escape. The building is surrounded by my people."

"This is outrageous!" Gentry blustered, watching three half-dressed men, who had been enjoying the fruits of the upstairs entertainment, hustled down the staircase and into the parlor.

Hunt made them sit on a couch with their pants wrapped around their ankles.

Gentry challenged, "This is illegal. I'm going to call the sheriff."

Mona said, "The sheriff is on the other side of town searching for an accident involving four cars, which he will never find. Besides all the telephones in the house are being dismantled."

Brezing glowered. "I wish you hadn't done that. I had a devil of a time getting the telephones installed in the first place."

"I'll make sure they are repaired after my business is concluded here."

"See that you do."

Gentry continued to complain and whine until Brezing said, "For goodness sake, shut up, Jacob. You've been had. Be a man and face it."

"Yes, indeed, you've lost, Mr. Gentry."

Gentry tugged on his suit coat. "I don't know what you mean."

Mona said gleefully, "Mr. Bludger has confessed to embezzling Moon Bank for you. We have signed documents of who, what, and when. What we don't know is where you've stashed the stolen funds."

"It's my word against Bludger's."

"Yes, it is, but once these photographs are leaked and word gets around that you are a regular in Belle's place, you can kiss any chance of being governor adios, especially since you were going to run on a moral ticket."

What Mona said was starting to sink into Gentry. "Look, I'm not an unreasonable man. Let's make a deal."

"I'm setting the conditions of the deal, not you."

"Agree to Miss Moon's demands, Jacob, or we'll all be ruined," encouraged one of Jacob's cohorts. "I have to protect my family."

"Should have thought about that before you visited a bawdy house," Mona snapped. "Men of your ilk use these poor girls and then rail against them. Worst type of hypocrite."

The man hung his head, saying nothing.

Mona said, "I want you to know that we will develop the film tonight, and glossy photographs will be ready to be distributed by morning."

"How?" Gentry asked. "All the photography studios are closed."

"Moon Enterprises has its own photography

lab in an undisclosed location. We use it to photograph all our documents, including patents. The drilling patent that Mr. Jeter stole had already been photographed and sent to the patent office weeks ago. I will assume that your presumed buyer of my patent will soon find out that it has already been submitted to the patent office and will come looking for a refund. I wouldn't want to be in your shoes."

Another of Gentry's cohorts complained, "Jacob, you told us this plan of yours was foolproof. You have landed us in the arms of the law. All we can do now is to ask for mercy."

Brezing laughed and clapped her hands. "Well done, Miss Moon. Well done. You have beaten these men at their own game." She hoisted her glass and gave Mona a small salute.

"This is blackmail, plain and simple," Gentry said.

"Blackmail versus theft, intimidation, manipulation, and then there's the matter of murder. Remember the death of Mr. Jones? The English solicitors were brought here by Hancock Jeter, who was taking orders from you, Mr. Gentry."

"Wait. Wait right now," complained Gentry's

compatriot, waving his finger at Mona. "We had nothing to do with that man's death. Absolutely nothing. I'll swear on the Bible to that."

The other men murmured to that effect.

"What happened?" Mona asked.

Gentry's compatriot answered, "We wanted Jeter to bring those English gents over to Belle's, so we made arrangements with him to bring them over. The Englishmen thought they were in a private gentlemen's club."

Another man spoke up. "Why were they in town? We knew they had something to do with Robert Farley, but didn't know what. We were just going to get them drunk and hopefully have them spill the beans. We didn't lay a hand on them. I swear none of us had anything to do with that young man's death."

"Yeah, you said that before, but I don't believe a word." Mona glanced at Brezing. "Nice crowd you run around with, Miss Belle," Mona said.

"It's a living," she replied, somewhat bored with the theatrics.

Gentry harrumped. "It doesn't matter what you say, Miss Moon. My pastor and church congregation will back me up no matter what."

Mona gave a sly smile. "I don't think so, Mr. Gentry. I will be at your church this coming Sunday service to give your pastor a hefty check to replace the roof and build a Sunday school addition."

Gentry gasped, "He wouldn't!"

"I'm afraid your pastor and I have reached an agreement to disagree on the place of women in the world. He and his wife are also having tea at my house on Saturday to discuss the final details of the allocation of the donated funds."

"That does it," several men chimed in. "Jacob, do anything this woman wants. We must save our reputations."

Mona said, "Yes, Jacob. I hold all the cards. Fold."

"What do you want?"

"You and your cohorts are to sign confessions, and they are to be witnessed by Miss Brezing and my attorney, Mr. Deatherage."

"Then we get the negatives and pictures?"

"No, Mr. Gentry, those negatives and pictures will be held by Moon Enterprises to ensure your good behavior. You haven't heard the rest of my conditions yet."

"Go on," Gentry sneered. He could hardly believe this young woman had gotten the better of him. It was humiliating.

"Monty Putnam is to write an apology to Violet Tate for his unbecoming behavior as well as one from your secretary to Miss Dotty. Both of their behaviors were appalling and not worthy of a gentleman."

"If you insist. Gentry pulled a cigar out of his coat pocket and bit the end off. "Go on."

"You and your associates agree to never run for any public office. I mean any office—even if it is for dog catcher."

"For how long?"

"Forever."

Jacob Gentry groaned, seeing his future political life ruined even before it got started.

"Now, where is my money?" Mona asked.

"I have a condition of my own."

"You are not in the position to make any stipulations."

Gentry forged ahead. "I want no further vendetta from you after we fulfill these conditions."

"I didn't start this war. You did."

"I don't want any leaks to our families. Nothing."

"Sign the confessions, tell me where my money is, and fulfill the conditions that I have set forth. We don't even need to speak when we see each other on the sidewalk." Mona motioned to Hunt to bring in Dexter.

Dexter entered the room and tipped his hat to Belle Brezing, who nodded back. If seeing half-naked men sitting on a couch with their pants wrapped around their ankles surprised him, Dexter didn't reveal it. Just a slight arch of his eyebrows conveyed his feelings.

Mona was playing a dangerous game and if she slipped, he would go down in flames with her. These men would not take being defeated by a woman lying down. Regardless, he had a job to do and put those thoughts behind him. Dexter laid the various documents and several ink pens on the poker table. "Sign here, please." He picked up a pen and handed it to Jacob Gentry.

With his hand shaking, Gentry signed the document.

"Date it as well, please, and write down your addresses," Dexter coaxed.

Gentry dated the document and handed the pen to Brezing. She signed with great flourish and dated the document. Then Dexter signed the document.

When done, Gentry fell into a chair, wondering where he had made his great mistake.

Dexter held out the pen and one-by-one Gentry's cabal signed the various confessions, including the partially clad men. Concluding his business, Dexter gathered the documents into his briefcase and left the premises.

Mona asked, "How is Melanie Moon tied up in this fiasco?"

Gentry shrugged. "Your aunt hates your guts for taking her place as matriarch of the Moon family. She's not directly involved, but Melanie might have whispered some sweet suggestions in my ear."

Mona felt queasy at the thought of Melanie cozying up to Gentry, trying to manipulate him. "Where is my money?" Mona asked.

Grinning, Gentry looked up at Mona. "That's one area where I outsmarted you. You'll never guess where I put it. It was right under your nose all the time, and you never even considered the possibility. It was so very clever."

Having new insight into the location of the missing money, Mona glanced at Hunt, grinning.

"Are you thinking what I am?"

Hunt's eyes widened. "Of course, The perfect place."

"Well, gentlemen, it seems our business has been concluded. I'll see you all in church this Sunday." Mona walked out of Belle Brezing's place with a renewed sense of purpose. She had fought back against male dominance and had won. She had butted her head against misogyny all her life. In fact, Mona had been turned down for an expedition to the Amazon simply because she was a woman on the very day Dexter knocked on the door of her New York tenement and announced the news of her uncle's death. Mona shook her head as she remembered that she had pulled a gun on Dexter much to his chagrin. Poor Dexter. She had certainly put him through the wringer.

Mona had the Amazon expedition rejection framed and hanging in her office to remind her of when the world was against her and she was so broke. Today was one of the few battles for her gender that Mona had won, and her uncle's money had made it possible. Maybe the world was changing for the better.

Mona certainly hoped so.

28

Mona and Hunt looked glumly at the rows and rows of deposit boxes in the cavernous vault of the Moon Bank.

"Are you sure the stolen money is in here?" Rupert asked, calculating how long it would take to search all the boxes before the bank opened.

"Gentry said it was right under our noses. It's like the *Purloined Letter* By Edgar Allan Poe."

"Never read it."

As Mona opened her mouth, Hunt rushed to say, "Please don't recount the story. Poe gives me nightmares."

Mona drew her lips between her teeth in an effort not to laugh. She couldn't imagine Rupert Hunt being afraid of anything.

"Bludger stole the money and gave it to Gentry. Gentry then gave the money to someone, most likely a lady, to hide the dole in a Moon Bank deposit box. Brilliant plan. I couldn't have done better myself."

"That's not comforting, Rupert."

"Look at the list. Maybe Gentry rented a box under his wife's name."

Mona scanned the list of deposit box holders in her hand. "No Gentry on the list."

"Look for a name that is goofy like Laura Lamoure or an anagram of some sort."

"I know most of these people. Nothing sticks out." Mona used her finger as a marker and reread each name out loud. "Wait a minute. Mira Hedge? Mira Hedge? There's that name again."

Hunt thought for a moment and then snapped his fingers. "She's the other gal at Belle's the night Mr. Jones was murdered."

"Of course," Mona said, exasperated. "Oh, dear."

"What's the matter?"

"I think I've dropped the ball with Mira Hedge. Belle warned me about her. I was so consumed with the banking issue that I forgot about Miss Hedge and she may be the key to this entire fiasco."

"Maybe the murder of Mr. Jones is connected to Miss Hedge, but first things first. Let's get that box open."

Mona handed Hunt the bank's master keys. "It's 213."

Hunt unlocked the deposit box's door and slowly swung it open. He then slid out the metal container and placed it on a table. "Cross your fingers, Mona."

Mona gently opened the lid. Both she and Hunt peered into the box.

Inside were rubber-banded stacks of lovely green legal tender.

Mona sighed with relief and silently thanked God for helping to recover her depositors' money.

Hunt dumped the money out on the table. "Help me count it."

Mona looked at her watch. They were running out of time. It wouldn't be long before newspaper boys, bakers, and the milkmen were up and about. The ice trucks would be rumbling on the streets as well.

Mona and Hunt grabbed stacks of money and began counting furiously. A half hour later, they finished.

Hunt looked at the total. "You're two thousand short."

"Mr. Bludger said he did a little dipping for himself. I'll write a check to cover the difference. If a bank auditor questions the discrepancy, I'll tell him that it was due to your incompetence as a teller, and that's why we had to fire you."

Hunt rolled his eyes beseechingly to the heavens. "Thank you, Lord. I have never had so tedious a job. You have released me from hell, good lady."

Mona placed the cash in the correct bank box used for daily business, closed the safe, and changed the tally in the official bank record minus the two thousand. Thinking she had covered all her tracks, she sent Hunt to fetch Dexter, who was now upstairs working in his office. Dexter came down the elevator with a briefcase.

"Mona, here are the negatives, pictures, and all the signed confessions. I think you should take this evidence and secure it at Moon Manor. Tell no one. Not even Dotty or Violet. Especially not Robert. He has such a filthy temper."

"You really think it necessary?"

"It is obvious that our security measures are inadequate. This isn't over. Those boys are not going to take this lying down. They will be looking for those photos. Until we get new security protocols in place, I think you should take this home with you."

"All right, but here is some good news." Mona explained that they had found the missing money.

"The clever buggers," Dexter said. "How are we going to explain the missing two thousand?"

Mona looked at Hunt, who curtsied. "If we are asked about that discrepancy by the banking commission, we are going to blame the theft on Rupert here."

Hunt teased, "Rupert Hunt is a cad, even if I say so myself."

Mona continued speaking, "If they catch on to the other missing funds, I'll tell them the money was misplaced into an empty deposit box, but never left the bank. It's pretty close to the truth. I will personally guarantee the missing money. I'll write a check later and have it delivered. Other than answering official inquiries, I want this kept hush hush from everyone else. I must keep the bank's reputation sterling to the public."

Dexter laughed. "We won't be the first bank to fiddle with the official records, but I think we are getting out of this jam by the skin of our teeth. I'll stay and explain things to the bank employees about Bludger getting a new position. It's almost dawn anyway. Whom do you wish to promote to bank manager? I think it should be in-house."

Mona offered, "Promote the loan officer. She lacks experience, but she's a hard worker and a quick learner. Here are the master keys to the vault and the deposit boxes."

"Okey dokey. You guys scoot. It will be light soon."

Mona took the briefcase and silently mouthed *thank you* to Dexter. "Come on Rupert. I'll drop you off at the train station."

"Where are you sending me now?"

"Out west to keep an eye on Bludger."

"It will be my pleasure, Mona."

Mona and Hunt left by the back door and climbed into a waiting car driven by Pinkertons.

The sun was just peeking over the horizon.

29

Mona was working in her office when Dotty came in holding a handwritten letter.

"May I speak with you?"

Mona laid down her pen and waved to a chair positioned in front of the desk. "What's on your mind?"

Dotty sat down, pulling her dress over her knees. "I wish to apologize. I've been frightfully rude to you for something that was not even your fault." She handed Mona the letter.

Quickly scanning the letter, Mona returned it. "It looks as though your former beau is confessing that he was ordered to become your acquaintance and ferret out information for his boss."

"You warned me, but I didn't take heed. I was stupid."

"Taken for a fool? I've been there, believe me."

Dotty shifted uneasily in her seat. "I want you to know that I am very grateful for the opportunities you have given me, and I do believe in the work you do. What do you always say? Money is like manure and should be spread around."

"What do you wish to do, Dotty?"

"I'd like to stay, if you will have me. I never intentionally leaked any information."

"But you had documents in your cottage and in your purse, which this man could have seen. You must be more careful. Anyone can insert themselves into our lives and make things difficult. We must always be on guard. Surely, you must realize this to be a fact of life if you work for me."

"How do you live like that? Always on your guard. It must be exhausting."

"I do trust people. I trust Mr. Thomas. I trust Mr. Deatherage. I trust Violet. I used to trust you."

"But you have doubts about me now?"

"Frankly, I do."

"I've learned my lesson. I would like to stay."

Mona leaned back in her chair, considering Dotty's request. "I have discovered that giving people second chances usually flies in the face of common sense."

"You gave Rupert Hunt a second chance after he had kidnapped you."

Mona was flummoxed. "You are right. I hired a thief and a kidnapper."

"Before Mr. Gentry sent his young assistant into my life, I was very content. I don't know what happened."

"I experienced betrayal with my first secretary, Jetta. She fell heels over in love with a man and lost all sense of herself. She put everyone who lived here in danger. I can't afford that again, Dotty. I'm not blaming you for dating this young man. I am worried that you don't seem to be angry about being used and won't take responsibility for being careless."

"You are in love. Surely you can understand my feelings."

"That's the problem, Dotty. I do understand. That's what makes this so difficult. Love can make a person do such foolish things. I need someone who is a little more circumspect. You were old enough to know better."

"Violet was in the same circumstances."

"Violet has never had a beau before this Monty Putnam. She just finished high school and is an innocent, sheltered girl. The bottom line is you seem to think this is my fault. I can't afford to employ people who have a grudge against me, real or imagined."

Dotty implored, "Please, Mona. I have no elsewhere to go. Don't make me beg."

Mona knew what is it was to be down on one's luck and jobs were hard to find, especially for women. Against her better judgment, Mona said, "You may stay, but next time you wish to date someone, have Dexter check him out first. I can't have another slip up."

Dotty stood. "I'm very grateful. You won't be sorry."

"I better not be."

Dotty waited.

"Is there anything else?"

"His Grace left a message for you."

"Robert did?" Mona looked around her desk. "Where's the message?"

Dotty lifted Mona's telephone to reveal a note.

"I must have accidentally scooted it under the telephone," Mona said. She stopped before she opened it. "When was this delivered?"

"Last evening. You weren't here."

"Yes, I was out with the Deatherages," Mona said, giving a false impression of her actions last night. "It's near lunchtime. Go get something to eat."

Dotty, understanding that Mona wanted to read the note alone, acquiesced and left the room.

As soon as the office door was closed, Mona tore open the envelope and read the note with Robert's handwriting scrawled across it.

Darling,

Jellybean called and has some news. Going to meet him. Don't know when I'll be back.

My love always, Robert.

Mona burned the note in an ashtray before calling Robert's home.

His phone rang and rang and rang.

30

Mona called the Deatherage home to see if Dexter had any contact with Robert or Jellybean Martin in the last thirty-six hours. Willie answered the phone telling Mona that Dexter was asleep, and she was not going to wake him. Willie would have him call when he awoke.

Though frustrated, she knew Dexter was exhausted and decided not to push the issue. She now regretted sending Rupert Hunt out west. She could have used him now. Mona decided the best thing she could do was wait. Robert was a big boy who could take care of himself. Mona pushed the fact that he had been recently attacked out of her mind. He had been ambushed, plain and simple. Robert would be more careful now.

Mona called to Chloe and went outside for a swim and a read. Chloe loved the water and Mona enjoyed throwing a ball for her in the pool. The standard poodle would happily have played this game for hours, but Mona grew tired and helped Chloe out of the water. Drying off, she went to sit in one of the yellow and white striped canvas lounging chairs.

Mona picked up her book and tried to read. She was finishing a Dorothy L. Sayers mystery which she had put aside previously due to her Washington visit and current events. While she had enjoyed meeting Eleanor Roosevelt on her trip to the nation's capital, the occasion at the White House had been less than stellar. In fact, the food had been awful.

Remembering the luncheon, Mona smiled at the thought of Alice Roosevelt Longworth sparring with her cousin, Eleanor at the luncheon. It had been a month ago, but seemed like she had been in Washington just yesterday. The events of the past weeks had been so chaotic, they passed as though a blur. Mona blinked and shook her head to shake random thoughts from her mind. She needed to concentrate. She tried to read, but her mind kept wandering off. Mona must have reread the same paragraph several times over before making sense of it. She put the book down in disgust and petted Chloe, who had snuggled beside her in the chair.

"Let's take a nap," she said to Chloe. She had just closed her eyes when Chloe growled and then barked furiously, jumping from the chaise lounge. Mona sprang up and saw Robert walking toward her. "Robert! Robert!" She ran to him.

He picked Mona up and swung her around. Looking down at his damp suit, he cheerfully complained, "You're getting me wet, Mona."

"We had just been swimming."

Robert put Mona down and bent over to pet Chloe, who was joyfully jumping up on him. "My goodness, what a reception. I should go away more often."

Mona stamped her foot. "Where have you been? I've been worried sick."

"Here we go again—that temper of yours."

"I didn't know if you had been kidnapped or thrown off a horse," Mona protested.

"Now, Mona, I left you a note that I was with Jellybean Martin."

Mona hugged Robert tightly. "Given Jelly-bean's penchant for getting into trouble, your note was hardly reassuring. I'm glad you are okay. What a load off my mind. You're fine. You're fine," she repeated, patting his chest.

Robert kissed the top of Mona's head. "Now, that's more like it. I've got lots to tell you, so come along. Gather your shoes and robe. Let's go to my house. No one is there, and I can tell you my story in peace."

"Let me run and tell Samuel where I'll be and not to disturb us."

"I'll be waiting here. Be a minute—no longer. I haven't properly kissed you yet."

Mona blew a kiss at him and ran to an open window where she saw Violet mending a dress. "Violet! Violet!"

Violet came to the window and peered out. "Yes, Miss Mona."

"His Grace is back and I'll be at his house. I don't want to be disturbed. Tell Monsieur Bisaillon to not cook anything special for tonight. Chloe will be with me."

"I'll tell him right now."

"Thank you." Mona ran back to a waiting

Robert with open arms. They both scampered to Robert's house with a delighted Chloe running beside them.

Mona was so happy, she felt she could fly. She was young and in love.

What could possibly go wrong?

31

Mona showered and dressed in a pair of Robert's trousers and pinstriped shirt. She pulled at the waist as tightly as she could with a woven cloth belt, but the pants felt dangerously loose as though they would fall down at any moment. She looked in the mirror at herself and giggled. The arms of the shirt were too long and had to be rolled up. Her face was clean of makeup and her hair was untidy. Mona felt glorious.

She came downstairs into the kitchen where Robert was making grilled cheese sandwiches for them. "Where did you learn to cook?"

"I can make simple things. Had to learn during my days in the army or else it was canned sausages every day." He lifted the browned sandwiches from the frying pan onto two plates and put them on the kitchen table. "Coffee?"

"Milk if you have it. If not, then water."

Robert looked in the icebox. "Hey, we've got some." He lifted the bottle's cardboard tab and sniffed. "Still good." He poured Mona a glass and then put the milk by her plate.

"How do you feel, Robert? I see most of the bruising has gone away."

"Still a little stiff around the shoulder, but nothing I can't handle."

"You said you had something to tell me."

"Yes." Robert went to a drawer and pulled out a certificate and a photograph, handing the certificate to Mona.

She wiped her greasy fingers on a napkin before picking the document up and looking at it curiously. "This is the birth certificate of Mira Hedge. Born 1903."

"Once you said Belle Brezing warned you about her, I hired Jellybean to track her down."

Mona chortled. "So have I."

"That little rascal. We've both been paying him double."

"What did you find?"

"She's the only witness on the night of Mr.

Jones' murder whom we have not interviewed."

"Did you speak with her?"

"Jellybean found relatives living in a shotgun house in Adamstown deeded to Mira."

"And?"

"Look closely at the birth certificate."

Mona studied the document. "Her mother was black and father is listed as unknown."

"You know what that means, don't you?"

"Not really."

"In this case, it's a euphemism for the father being white."

Mona lay the certificate down. "I don't know what you are implying here."

"Jellybean discovered that Mira's mother was Seraphina Hedge, a black woman who worked for Belle Brezing."

"It says on the certificate that her mother was Sara Hedge."

Robert tapped the document. "Seraphina was her "working" name."

"Oh, I see."

"Jellybean talked to Mira's relatives in Adamstown and discovered that Seraphina was highly prized by Brezing and worked several years until a white man fell in love with her. They ran off together and Seraphina had a baby. The white man abandoned her and denied all knowledge of the child. Seraphina died shortly thereafter from typhoid, and the man gave the child to Brezing, who took care of her."

Mona finished the tale. "And raised her to become a whore. That's a really disgusting story."

"That's not all. Jellybean got a picture of Mira Hedge from her cousin." He put the photograph in front of Mona.

She stared at a light-skinned girl wearing a wool coat with fur trim, a Cloche hat with a feather in the rim, and black leather gloves. The young lady was smiling with perfectly straight teeth and clear skin, looking happy. "She's so young in this picture. Maybe sixteen or seventeen."

"Mira was fifteen. It's written on the back."

Mona turned the picture over and noted the cursive handwriting. It was flowery with bold flourishes. She had seen that handwriting before. It was Belle Brezing's handwriting.

"Who does Mira Hedge look like?"

Mona studied the picture and came to a realization. "Oh, good Lord. She looks like Jacob Gentry." Mona felt faint. "He turned his own daughter over to a notorious madam to raise." She pushed her plate away. "I've lost my appetite. I'm not hungry any longer."

"You know what I think we should do?"

"I hope you can think of something positive to do because my mind is addled."

"I think we should pay a visit to Miss Belle."

"I think you're right. I'll be ready in thirty minutes. Have the car running? Come, Chloe. Come. We must make haste," Mona said, before rushing out the door.

Robert watched Mona jump the hedge that divided their properties. He hoped that once Mr. Jones' murder was solved, he could get things back on track with Mona.

It could be his imagination, but Robert felt Mona was slipping away.

32

Mona and Robert were shown into the library, where Brezing sat in a dark blue beaded dress. Her hair was swept up in a bun with diamond pins.

"Miss Moon, I see that you've brought your fiancé with you to visit. I thought I had seen the last of you darkening my doorstep. You were fit to be tied when last we met."

"I'm glad you found my anger amusing."

"I never said that nor did I give that impression."

"You let Jacob Gentry plan his schemes against me in your parlor. I take offense to that."

"You should know by now that one way to survive in my business is to *mind* my own business. However, I sprinkled bread crumbs for you to follow."

Robert extended his hand. "Miss Belle, I am Robert Farley. I did follow the breadcrumbs and wondered if you can set us straight on some questions."

Brezing shook his hand. "Do you mind if I smoke? It calms my nerves."

Both Mona and Robert shook their heads.

"Please sit down." After Brezing offered them a cigarette, she lit one herself and drew deeply, blowing smoke out her nose. "Actually, I've been expecting you. Ask away."

Robert spread out Mira Hedges' birth certificate and picture.

Brezing picked up Mira's picture and studied it. "Wasn't she a pretty young thing?"

"We think Jacob Gentry is her father. We see a resemblance around the eyes and mouth."

"Very good. Yes, Jacob is her father. Met her mother, Seraphina, here twenty-one years ago."

"Was Seraphina a working girl?" Robert asked.

Belle nodded. "One of my best girls. She really brought in the clientele. Seraphina was considered exotic."

"What happened?" Robert asked.

"I told Seraphina that Jacob was no good, but she was enthralled that a white boy had fallen in love with her. Have you ever heard of the expression—empty wagons make a lot of noise? That is Jacob Gentery, but at the time, he was nineteen, good-looking, and came from a well-to-do family. She thought his obsession with her was the real thing, poor fool. As usual, my advice went unheeded. She ran off with Jacob, thinking he would marry her, but all he wanted to do is to sow some wild oats. As soon as Jacob was bored, he jumped ship, but Seraphina was pregnant by then."

Mona asked, "Where did they run to?"

"New Orleans, of all places. When Jacob returned and I didn't see Seraphina around town, I knew he had deserted her. I sent a private detective to Louisiana looking for her. He found Seraphina broke, both financially and in spirit. She was brought here, and I took care of her until the baby was born. After that, she went back to work for me, but it wasn't the same. The fire in her eyes was out."

"Maybe it was because she was whoring for you," Mona spat out.

"That may be true, Miss Moon, but I was also provided a salary, two meals a day, clean sheets, and a roof over her head. This was 1903. There weren't many alternatives of employment for women then—not the kind of money she was making. But you're right, Seraphina didn't like the business. She wanted out and was saving money for her escape."

Robert asked, "What happened to the baby?"

"She was sent away to live with a wet nurse. When she got older, I sent her to a boarding school."

"But Mira had family in Adamstown," Robert said. "Couldn't they have cared for her?"

"She was just another mouth to feed for a beleaguered population. Surely, you understand what I'm talking about."

Robert and Mona glanced at each other. This conversation was putting Brezing in a softer light.

Mona was curious. "Did Mira ever see her mother?"

"Of course. Seraphina saw her every chance she could, but it wasn't often. Then Seraphina came down with typhoid. She didn't fight the disease. It was like she welcomed death. But I don't think she died because of typhoid. I think Seraphina died of a broken heart."

Mona said, "It sounds like you cared for this woman, and yet, you allow Jacob Gentry to use your home to destroy this woman's life."

"Is that what you think? I've been waiting years for someone to take him down."

"Why didn't you take Gentry down?" Mona asked.

Brezing jeered, "And have every law enforcement officer within a hundred mile radius come after my scalp? No thank you. I needed a champion with more money and clout than I had. I let Jacob play cards here, so I could keep an eye on him."

"Miss Belle has a point, Mona," Robert offered, prompting a spiteful look from Mona. Robert turned to the madam who was stubbing out her cigarette in an ashtray. "So what is Mira's story?"

"Mira stayed in boarding school until she showed up at my doorstep one evening. I tried to coax her to go back to school, but she said she was done. I finally called the school and found out that Mira had been expelled. The school said her conduct was unacceptable, but wouldn't give me examples. Later I discovered that Mira had intercepted a letter from them informing me of her dismissal."

"Is that when you put her to work for you?" Mona asked.

Brezing gave Mona a scorching look. "No, Miss Moon. I have never forced anyone to work for me, besides Mira never worked as one of my girls. She was my ward. I tried everything to get Mira to go to another school to finish her education, but the longer she stayed here, the more concerned I became."

"In what way?" Robert asked.

Brezing sighed and said softly, "Mira began displaying disturbing behavior."

Robert and Mona waited for Brezing to compose her thoughts.

"Mira complained of headaches and scratched herself raw saying there were bugs crawling on her skin. Then she began laughing uncontrollably at odd moments. The final straw was when Mira bit the maid changing the sheets on her bed. It was a bad bite. When I searched her room, I found two kitchen knives. That's when I became convinced that something was really wrong with Mira and that she was a danger."

Robert sat on the edge of his chair. "What did you do, Miss Belle?"

"I had one of the best doctors from Cincinnati visit and observe Mira. He believed she was seriously ill and needed to be admitted to Eastern State Hospital for psychiatric treatment. She was to be admitted the following week." Belle teared up and her voice cracked. "We weren't quick enough."

"What do you mean, Miss Belle?" Robert asked, already guessing the answer.

Mona knew the truth too, but wanted Belle to utter it.

Brezing looked squarely at Robert. "Mira killed your solicitor, Mr. Jones."

"Why?"

"You must ask her. She is at Eastern State Hospital."

Mona said, "Why didn't you tell the sheriff?"

"I wasn't sure at the time. I thought Sally might have done it. She has a violent temper."

"What made you change your mind, Miss Belle?" Robert asked.

"I called Sheriff Monahan and he told me the approximate time of the death. There was no way Sally could have killed Mr. Jones. She was serving drinks downstairs at that time. We had an all-nighter of card playing."

"Have you confronted Mira about the murder?" Mona asked.

"No. I don't think my heart could stand it if she confessed to me. I'm too old to hear such confessions now." There was silence in the room until Brezing spoke again. "I can call and ask them to allow you both to see her."

Robert insisted, "Yes, we need to clear up the matter of Mr. Jones' death. I have two British subjects anxious to get home to their families."

"I have one last question. Does Gentry know Mira is his daughter?" Mona asked.

"If he does, he has never mentioned it or showed any sign of recognition."

"Does Mira know Jacob Gentry is her father?"

"I hope to the good Lord not, but I have no idea what Seraphina may have revealed to Mira."

Robert stood. "I think we have taken up too much of your time. Thank you for seeing us, Miss

Belle. You have been more than forthcoming."

"I'm sorry that I couldn't help you on the night of your assault. By the time Jacob's boys dropped your car off the deed was already done, but I did call the authorities."

"I don't recall the police finding me."

"They don't always come when I call. It's a fact of life here in this neighborhood."

Mona stood as well. "Thank you."

Brezing addressed Mona. "My dear, I know you think me heartless and a schemer, but don't judge me too harshly. We are cut from the same bolt of cloth, you and I."

Mona didn't respond, but thought Brezing might be correct. After all, she'd had opportunities that were out of Brezing's grasp when young. The infamous madam had done the best she could with the prospects that came her way. Finally, Mona said, "I'd like to hear about old Lexington one day."

Brezing brightened. "Yes, indeed, and remember we are to discuss books."

After a maid handed Mona her hat and gloves, Mona followed Robert out on the porch stoop. "It's never simple, is it?"

"No. Never." He wrapped Mona's arm around his and escorted her to the car. They had a stop to make before heading for the hospital.

33

Mona, Robert, Dexter, Sheriff Monahan, and a stenographer entered the guarded gates of Eastern State Hospital. When Mira's doctor saw the entourage, he forbade a meeting with Mira, saying she was too fragile to meet with them. Sheriff Monahan pulled rank and threatened the doctor with arrest since he was impeding a murder investigation.

Understanding the doctor's concern, Mona quieted the sheriff and requested that she see Mira alone with the stenographer close enough to hear. Sheriff Monahan hesitated until Mona asked him to write down questions he would ask. Relenting, Monahan wrote down ten questions he would ask Mira, if allowed.

"All right, Miss Moon, but I want a record of

everything that is said."

"I'll try to be a good detective, Sheriff," Mona replied.

After twenty minutes of preparation, the group was allowed into the main population of patients. They entered the visitation room where the stenographer set her machine up nearby while Mona sat at a table with a checkerboard set up. Robert and Sheriff Monahan sat in a row of chairs near a wall.

Mona waited until Mira entered the cavernous visitation room, escorted by a nurse who led her over. "Mira, you have a visitor."

The young woman took one look at Mona and recoiled. "I don't know her. Take me back to my room." Mira pointed a finger at Mona. "She's a witch. Look at her hair."

Mona stood. "Mira, I'm a friend of Belle's. She sent me. I know the color of my hair may frighten people, but the color runs in my family. There's nothing I can do about it." Mona tugged on her hair. "You can touch my hair, if you like. It won't hurt you."

The nurse coaxed, "Mira, you like Jean Harlow, don't you? You've seen her pictures. This lady looks like Jean Harlow. You don't call Miss Harlow a witch."

Mona studied the shy, wide-eyed woman before her. She was nicely dressed in a fresh summer frock, but wore no stockings and house slippers instead of shoes. Mona guessed that the lack of stockings and shoes was a hospital rule. She noted that Mira's nails were painted and her hair was combed in the latest style. It was obvious that Mira was being well-cared for.

Mona picked up a box of chocolates she had brought with her. "I've brought chocolates with me." She opened the box and held it out. "Would you like one?"

Mira looked at the box with distrust and clung to the nurse.

"Nurse, would you like a chocolate?" Mona asked, holding the candy box out to her.

"I don't mind if I do." The nurse took a chocolate nugget and popped it in her mouth. "See, Mira. Nothing to worry about. Have a seat here and I'll come back for you in a few minutes."

Mona put the box on the table. "Nurse, perhaps Mira would feel more comfortable if you sat with us."

The nurse looked at her watch. "I have other patients."

"I know, but it is very important that Mira feel comfortable with me."

"All right, if you insist, but you must speak up if I get into trouble for lollygagging." The nurse sat down and had another piece of candy.

Mona pushed the box toward the young girl. "Please Mira. Have a candy. There's toffee in the box. I understand you like toffee."

"I do very much. Thank you." Overcoming her reluctance, Mira reached for the toffee.

"Mira, my name is Mona Moon. I'd like to ask you a few questions." Mona turned to see if the stenographer was listening. The stenographer gave a thumbs up.

"What do you want to know?"

"Do you remember a girl named Sally who worked at Belle Brezing's place?"

Mira found a toffee and picked it up. "Yes, I didn't like her." She popped the candy into her mouth and chewed slowly.

"Why is that?"

"Because all the boys liked her and not me."

"You're so pretty I bet lots of boys adore you."

Mira smiled at Mona before she ate another toffee.

Mona continued, "But Sally worked at Belle's. She was employed to entertain customers. You were Belle's ward and not expected to work there."

The nurse leaned forward, hoping not to miss a word of the conversation. Although she knew Mira was Belle Brezing's ward, she wanted to hear the salacious goings on in that house of sin.

"Yes, but I liked to talk to the men, especially the college boys who come, but they always wanted to talk with Sally."

Mona's brow creased. "I thought Belle was retired and only let old customers come inside."

"Sometimes she'd let new people come in if they had the right credentials. She liked to meet people, too, you know. We both get lonely."

"I see. Did you meet a Mr. Jones there? He was British."

"Yes, he liked Sally too much. I wanted to talk with him about Europe. I was especially interested in European politics, but he ignored me, making google eyes at Sally. Made me mad and I said so."

"What happened then?"

"He blew me off and went upstairs with Sally."

"How did that make you feel?"

"Angry."

"How angry?"

"Very, but I got him back."

"How was that?"

Mira proudly said, "I got an ice pick from the kitchen and when Sally left the room, I went inside and stabbed him. He was asleep and didn't hear me."

"Are you sure you stabbed him?"

"Oh, yes. Right where the heart is located."

"Was the man's name Mr. Jones?"

Mira shrugged and chewed on her lip. "I don't know. He sounded strange. That's how I knew he was from England. From his accent, you know. There were two other men with him. They spoke hoity-toity like him."

"After you stabbed the man, what did you do?"

"Got ready for breakfast. I could smell bacon frying."

"Did you feel bad for hurting Mr. Jones?"

"No. Should I have?" Mira looked between the nurse and Mona for an answer.

The nurse interrupted. "I think that is enough. You have what you need."

"I think you're right. Thank you." Mona turned her attention to Mira. "Thank you for speaking with me, Mira."

"May I keep the chocolates?"

"Of course."

Mira grabbed Mona's arm. "Is Belle coming to see me?"

Mona calmly removed her arm from Mira's strong grip. "I'm sure she will come to see you as soon as she can. I have to go now."

"Okay. Nice to have met you."

"Same here." Mona watched the nurse lead Mira away. After speaking with the stenographer, Mona went over to Sheriff Monahan and Robert, who were waiting anxiously.

"Well?" asked the sheriff.

"My employee will type up her notes and deliver them to your office within two hours."

"Did she do it?"

"Yes, Sheriff, she did, but I really think she is not in her right mind. You may have to wait on her arrest."

Robert asked, "Can my men go back to England now?"

"Once I get the transcript and make an official determination, then yes. I'll call and let you know."

"May we drop you off, Sheriff?" Mona asked.

"I have my own car. Wait for my call, Farley," the sheriff said, before leaving.

Mona looked up at Robert, who had an agitated look about him. "What's the matter? We discovered the killer. We are in the clear."

"No 'Mr. Farley.' No 'Lord Farley.' No 'Duke' salutation. No sign of respect from that man."

"Robert, you're concerned over how Americans address you when a girl's life is ruined?"

"Stupid, isn't it? The ego of men. How did we become such vain creatures, Mona? Of course, I am relieved now that I can send those lawyers back home and get on with our lives."

"We survived with our reputations intact. We won the day, so why I don't feel happy?"

Robert said, "I talked with Mira's doctor briefly. They are going to try a new treatment tomorrow—insulin therapy. He said he was very hopeful about the results."

"Surely a jury wouldn't hold Mira responsible. She clearly wasn't of sound mind when she killed Mr. Jones."

"Come darling. We need to think about ourselves now. Let's go have one last talk with the solicitors and get our lives back on track." Robert escorted Mona from the visitor's room, shaking off all that sadness.

Poor Mira Hedge. Mona prayed for her on the way home. Life was so unfair. Sometimes Mona felt overwhelmed by it.

34

Two weeks later, Mona, Violet, and Willie were in the the dining room, licking linen envelopes that held an invitation to a party at Moon Manor. Dotty was busy writing addresses on them as she had the best handwriting of all four women.

After consulting an Emily Post book on etiquette, Violet asked, "Is this really an engagement party?" She slid an invitation into an envelope and sealed it with wax.

"That's the plan," Mona replied, "unless something goes wrong. Then we'll just have a nice party."

"What can go wrong?" Violet kidded.

All four woman twittered.

"Nothing, I hope," Mona said.

"What are you going to do with out-of-town

guests? I'm sure Mrs. Longworth will come," Willie said, looking unhappily at the stack of envelopes before her.

"I'll put everyone at the hotel in town."

"If you do announce your engagement, where and when will the wedding be?" Dotty asked.

"Haven't decided yet. Let's get the engagement announced, and then I'll worry about the marriage ceremony," Mona answered cheerfully. Since she had boxed in Aunt Melanie and Jacob Gentry and his cohorts, Mona felt as though she could float, hoping the worst was behind her and Robert. "I will tell you this, I have picked out a wedding dress pattern and Violet is going to make it for me."

Willie gushed, "Oh, Violet, that is wonderful. It will be the making of you. After everyone sees Mona's dress, they will want you to sew for them."

"It's always been my dream to open my own dress shop, but I don't think I'm ready right now," Violet said modestly.

"When a door opens, walk through it," Willie advised. "You might not get another shot. That's just the way life is."

Violet nodded.

Not listening to the chatter, Mona admired the off-white invitations. Was it really true? Was she going to announce her marriage to Robert Farley?

Out of the corner of her eye, she spied Samuel walking toward her with a silver tray. It was the letter tray. It must be important if Samuel brought it out to her instead of putting the mail on her desk.

While the other ladies were chatting away, Samuel solemnly presented the tray to Mona. On it was a telegram. Mona knew from Samuel's grim expression that it was not good. Not that Samuel would steam open the telegram and read it before resealing it, but Monsieur Bisaillon would and then tell the staff. "Thank you, Samuel. You can go."

"What is it, Mona?" Willie asked, dripping wax on her envelope and pressing the Moon seal into it.

"I don't know." Mona tore open the envelope and read quickly, after which she let the telegram flutter from her fingers.

Anxious, Willie picked up the telegram and

read it out loud.

Mona. STOP Coming home. STOP Found the man of my dreams. STOP I want you to throw a party for me to announce my new fiancé. STOP Going on that cruise was a great idea. STOP Thought you'd be surprised. STOP Maybe we can have a double wedding. STOP Arriving on the 27th. STOP Aunt Melanie

Dotty, Willie, and Violet turned to Mona.

Willie said, "Of all the gall. She's trying to steal your thunder."

"The 27th is two days from now." Violet said.

Mona laughed. "Don't fret, ladies. I've dealt with hombres tougher than Melanie."

Violet asked, "What are you going to do, Miss Mona?"

Mona smiled at Violet. "What all ladies do in this situation? Plan around the distraction. Let's get back to the invitations, ladies. I have a party to plan."

Violet, Dotty, and Willie straggled back to the table to resume their work, while Mona left to walk in her garden, wondering. How was she ever going to be happy with Melanie nipping at her heels all the time?

"Mona?"

Mona looked up and saw Robert standing on a garden path, pensively staring at her.

"What are you doing out here?" he asked. "Shouldn't you be helping with the invitations?"

"I came out here to think."

"About what?"

She waved at Moon Manor. "Wondering if all this grandeur is worth the fight. I try to do the right thing, but I keep getting hammered for it."

Robert went to Mona and held her in his arms. "Let me make this easy for you. I release you from your promise to marry me."

Mona pulled away. "What are you saying, Robert? You don't want me anymore?"

"I'm a distraction from the work you wish to do. I will drink again, Mona. I feel the desire gnawing at my insides. I don't know if I have the strength to fight it. I'm worried that I'll drag you down in the end. That's just part of my concern. There's going to be a war in Europe."

"I don't believe it. Hitler is all bluster."

"I hope you're right, but if there is another

war, I'll volunteer to fight again."

"You're too old. The military wouldn't want you."

"Don't you see what I'm saying, Mona. Marriage between us would be a relationship with long absences between us with your life over here and my life in England. You can't tell me you haven't thought of the disadvantages of us hitching our horses to the same wagon."

"Do you love me, Robert?"

"Madly. That's why I'm willing to give you up."

"I love you, too. Besides my parents, I have never loved anyone before you. I have thought about all the compromises I would have to make being your wife, but I'm willing. Let's plunge ahead and face the world and all its folly together."

"You mean it!"

Mona smiled and brushed Robert's hair from his forehead. "Yes, darling. Let's throw caution to the wind. We'll face everything together, and if war comes to England, we'll face that, too."

Robert embraced Mona and they stood locked together with Mona's head on Robert's shoulder.

Finally releasing each other, they spent the rest of the evening sitting in the garden and holding hands.

Mona knew she would never love like this again and made a wish on the evening star.

Please, God, guide our way into calm ports and help me to be wise.

She rose from her chair and pulled Robert inside Moon Manor. After all, they had party invitations to get out announcing to the world that they were engaged.

Adamstown

Adamstown was an African American neighborhood located at the edge of Lexington, Kentucky in the 1870s. There were fifty to seventy families living here. The neighborhood was razed to make room for the University of Kentucky's Memorial Coliseum on Euclid Avenue in 1949.

Alice Blue

Alice blue is a pale shade of gray-blue associated with Alice Roosevelt Longworth as it was her signature color. The song, *Alice Blue Gown*, premiered in the 1919 Broadway musical *Irene*. The color is used by the United States Navy for the insignia and trim on the USS Theodore Roosevelt.

Alice Roosevelt Longworth (1884-1980)

Alice was the eldest child of U.S. President Theodore Roosevelt. Interested in politics, she married Nicholas Longworth (Republican-Ohio) who was the Speaker of the U.S. House of Representatives from 1925 to 1931. Their marriage was unconventional, and both parties had affairs. Alice's only child, Paulina, was sired from an affair with Senator William Borah of

Idaho. Paulina died from an overdose in 1955, leaving Alice to raise her granddaughter. Known as a great wit, Alice is famous for saying, "If you haven't got anything nice to say about anybody, come sit next to me." She said of her father's need for attention, "My father always wanted to be the corpse at every funeral, the bride at every wedding, and the baby at every christening."

American Isolationism

A popular 1930s social and political philosophy advocating American non-involvement in foreign military conflicts, especially Europe and Asia.

Associated Press (1846—)

AP is a trusted source of information in all formats to the news business. It is an independent and global organization that provides unbiased information to news agencies.

Belle Brezing (Breezing) (1860-1940)

Belle Brezing was a famous madam of a "bawdy house" in Lexington, Kentucky. Brezing was compromised at the age of twelve by a man who was thirty-six with whom she had a two year affair. Twelve was the age of consent in Kentucky at that time. When fifteen, she got pregnant from one of several men she was seeing and married a James Kenney, who deserted her nine days after they were married. At sixteen and attending her mother's funeral, Brezing was locked out of her house by the landlord and her possessions were thrown into the street. The next day she went to work as a street prostitute. At the age of nineteen, she joined Jennie Hill's brothel located in Mary Todd Lincoln's childhood home before opening up her own house, known for its fine furnishings, good food, and excellent liquor. Her house of ill repute was considered one of the finest in the South, and she entertained many famous men. When arrested in 1882 for prostitution, she was given a pardon by Kentucky Governor, Luke P. Blackburn. Margaret Mitchell's husband, John Marsh, working as a reporter for the Lexington Leader, often had breakfast in Brezing's kitchen so he could listen to all the gossip. Many scholars think Brezing is the model for Mitchell's Belle Watling in *Gone with the Wind*. When Brezing died, Time Magazine published her obituary and the Lexington Herald published a front page eulogy. Her home was known as the "most orderly of disorderly houses." During my years at the University of Kentucky, Brezing's house was torn down and the bricks were sold to all comers. I wish I had purchased one.

Bessie Smith (1894-1937)

Nicknamed the Empress of the Blues, Smith was a popular American blues and jazz singer during the 1920s and 1930s. Smith recorded for Columbia Records. She died in a car crash at the age of 43 in 1937.

Blackjacks

A hand weapon used to hit people over the head. It is usually made with clay, lead powder, or bbs enclosed in a piece of leather. Could be carried in a pocket.

Cloche Hats

A cloche hat was a bell-shaped hat for women, invented by Caroline Reboux in 1908. They were popular from 1922 until the mid-thirties.

Cocaine and Laudanum Use Among Soldiers

During the Great War (WWI), cocaine was used by the military for medical use and as a perfor-mance enhancer. It was not a controlled substance and available to anyone. British friends and family were encouraged to buy kits titled "A Welcome Present for Friends at the Front" which contained cocaine, morphine, syringes, and needles. Even the soft drink, Coca-Cola, had cocaine in it until 1929.

Laudanum is a ten percent solution of opium powder in alcohol and is more closely associated with addicted American Civil War soldiers, but was still used in the early twentieth century for pain and everything else in between, including teething babies. By the late 1800s, women made up more than sixty percent of opium addicts. Oxycontin is not the first opiate epidemic the United States has experienced.

Dorothy L. Sayers (1893-1957)

Sayers was an English mystery writer best known for *The Nine Tailors,* featuring her protagonist, English aristocrat and amateur sleuth, Lord Peter Wimsey. She was also a classical scholar who translated Dante's *Divine Comedy.* Besides writing mysteries, Sayers wrote plays, poetry, and literary criticism. Although she distanced herself from feminism, *Gaudy Night* is considered the first feminist mystery, featuring Harriet Vane and Lord Peter Wimsey.

Dress to the Nines

This is an English idiom meaning "perfection." By the twentieth century, the phrase was commonly written or spoken in reference to attire such as "dressed to the nines" or "dressed up to the nines." It was first used in a poem from the 1719 *Epistle to Ramsay* by the Scottish poet, William Hamilton.

> *The bonny lines therein thou sent me,*
> *How to the nines they did content me.*

Eastern State Hospital (1817—)

Eastern State Hospital is located in Lexington, Kentucky. It was started in 1817 as the Fayette Hospital and, at one time, had over 2000 beds. It is the second oldest psychiatric hospital in the United States.

Edgar Allan Poe (1809-1849)

Before there were Stephen King and Dean Koontz, there was Edgar Allan Poe. He is considered one of the United States finest authors and best known for his poetry and short stories. Most of his stories deal with the macabre and Poe is considered to be the inventor of the detective fiction genre as well as a strong influence on horror and science fiction writing. Poe was one of the first American writers to make his living through writing alone. To honor Poe, the Mystery Writers of America give out the Edgar Award each year for notable work in mystery writing.

Eleanor Roosevelt (1884-1962)

Roosevelt served as First Lady of the United States from 1933 to 1945. During this time, Mrs. Roosevelt worked to expand the rights of working women, WWII refugees, and the civil rights of minorities. She advocated the U.S. join the United Nations and was appointed as its first delegate. Serving as first chair on the UN Commission on Human Rights, she oversaw the drafting of the Universal Declaration of Human Rights. Roosevelt later chaired President John Kennedy's Presidential Commission on the Status of Women. She was the niece of President Theodore Roosevelt and first cousin to Alice Roosevelt Longworth. Roosevelt married her fifth cousin once removed, Franklin Delano Roosevelt, who became the 32nd President of the U.S. She is considered one of the most admired people of the twentieth century.

Emergency Banking Act of 1933

People began withdrawing their savings from banks as the deposits were not government insured. (Many people kept their cash in a tin can buried in the back yard. My mother did.) This caused a nationwide panic in 1933 when bank customers were turned away because of a shortage of paper money and credit. Fearing that they would lose their life savings, people caused a run on all banks. This forced banks to liquidate loans and led to banks closing their doors. Between 1930 and 1933, 9000 banks closed with 4000 in 1933 alone. 1933 and 1934 were the worst years of the Great Depression.

On March 9th, 1933, President Franklin Roosevelt called a special session of Congress the day after his inauguration and declared a four-day banking holiday in order to shut down all banks and the Federal Reserve as well. Then he had Congress pass the Emergency Banking Act to restore confidence. When banks reopened on March 13th, many customers redeposited their cash because of the government's creation of the FDIC-Federal Deposit Insurance Corporation.

Emily Price Post (1872-1960)

Post was a wealthy socialite who wrote novels, travel books, and etiquette books. Her 1922 etiquette book, *Etiquette in Society, in Business, in Politics, and at Home,* became a bestseller and launched Post as an American icon. She became a national figure on deciding what "good taste" was. After 1931, Post did radio programs and newspaper columns on proper etiquette. *Etiquette in Society, in Business, in Politics, and at Home is* still in print.

English Solicitors vs Barristers

Solicitors basically negotiate and prepare legal documents. They do not argue in court. Barristers present on behalf of a client in front of a judge and wear a wig and gown in court.

Great Depression (1929-1941)

The Great Depression was a world-wide phenomenon caused by the U.S. stock market crash in October 1929. The years 1933-1934 were the worst years of the Depression. The economy got better by 1939, but the United States didn't come roaring out from the Depression until 1941.

Great War

We now refer to the war in Europe from 1914 to 1918 as WWI.

Henrietta Nesbitt (1888-1963)

Nesbitt was hired by Eleanor Roosevelt as a housekeeper and cook for the White House. The two of them modernized the White House kitchen, thus upgrading its sanitary standards. Mrs. Roosevelt worked with Mrs. Nesbitt to create dishes that were nutritious and inexpensive. The First Lady believed the White House should provide an example during the Great Depression and eat what the "people" ate. Lavish meals, even for State dinners, became a thing of the past in favor of more spartan meals. While nutritious, Mrs. Nesbitt's meals were not tasty, and the White House became known for its inedible food. The rule of thumb was to eat before you dined at the White House.

Hobos

Usually men of all ages who were forced to leave home and look for work or food. They were known to ride the railways.

Horatio Nelson, 1ˢᵗ Viscount Nelson, 1ˢᵗ Duke of Bronté (1758-1805)

Nelson was regarded as one of the greatest commanders, if not the greatest English naval commander in history. Nelson saved Great Britain from being invaded by Napoleon Bonaparte at the Battle of Trafalgar on October 20th, 1805, during which Nelson was shot in the back and mortally wounded. His last words were, "God and my country."

Iceboxes

Iceboxes, also called cold closets, were kitchen aids to help keep food from spoiling. They had hollow walls, which were lined with tin or zinc and packed with various insulating materials such as cork, sawdust, or straw. A large block of ice was held in a tray or compartment near the top of the box. Ice blocks could also be put on the bottom shelf and food placed on shelves above. The ice would eventually melt into a pan and would be replaced with a new block of ice by the "iceman" who would come to the house several times a week or once weekly. The icebox largely disappeared as a household appliance in the 1950s as almost everyone could now afford an electric/motorized refrigerator. Old timers still refer to a refrigerator as an "icebox."

Insulin Therapy

Insulin Therapy was considered a breakthrough treatment for psychosis. In 1927, a Polish neurophysiologist, Manfred Sakel, induced a morphine-addicted woman into a coma through the use of insulin. When revived, the woman made a remarkable recovery. Sakel went on to induce convulsions in patients using insulin as a form of shock therapy. This therapy had such positive results it was used for decades until more modern therapy took its place.

Jack Benny (1894-1974)

Jack Benny was a popular radio and TV American entertainer, who was known for his comic timing. Benny's public persona emphasized him as a miser, a terrible violin player, and a liar about his age, which he always claimed to be 39 regardless of his real age. In fact, he was an accomplished violin player and generously donated to charities. Benny was known to cause laughter with a bewildered expression, a pause, or his signature line, "Well!"

Jaeger-LeCoultre Reverso

The Reverso was and still is a much sought after wristwatch from Swiss luxury watch manufacturer Jaeger-LeCoultre.

Jazz

Jazz is a variety of music originated by African-American musicians in New Orleans, Louisiana around the turn of the 20ᵗʰ century. It was considered controversial when it spilled over into the white population as it was rumored to have begun in houses of ill repute. Jazz has its roots in ragtime and the blues.

Jean Harlow (1911-1937)

Harlow was an American comedic actress and one of the first sex symbols of the "talkies." Known as the "Platinum Bombshell," she became one of Hollywood's biggest stars and is still ranked at No. 22 on AFI's greatest female stars of the Golden Age of Hollywood. Harlow died of kidney failure at the age of twenty-six.

Jezebel (Circa 850 B.C.E. or A. D.)

Jezebel is a label with sexual connotations given to any rebellious woman. In sacred texts, Jezebel was a Phoenician princess and priestess for the mother-goddess Astarte and her consort Baal. She was the daughter of Ithobaal I, king of Tyre (1 Kings 16:31) and married King Ahab of Samaria, who worshipped Yahweh. The two systems of worship and culture conflicted and came to a crisis when Jezebel arranged for the murder of Naboth, so Ahab could confiscate the man's vineyards. A war ensued and the Yahweh faction won. Ahab and his successors were killed as they were deemed unfit to rule, and Jezebel was thrown to her death out of a window where dogs ate her corpse just as the Yahweh prophet, Elijah, prophesied.

Johnny Cook (circa 1855-1875)

He was a possible lover of Belle Brezing. In 1875, Cook was shot in the head near Brezing's home nine days after she married Cook's friend, James Kenney. During those nine days, Brezing had written to Cook twice, the last note being in his pocket when examined by the coroner.

Dear One,

I will be downtown at three o'clock. Look out

for me. I will go to the office and by the store. Ma has come. Have my pistol for me. Belle

Brezing's husband, James Kenney, left town and did not return for ten years. Johnny Cook's death was listed as a suicide, but most people think it was murder.

Kentucky Burgoo

Burgoo is a hardy stew made from any meats and vegetables available. There is no set recipe. In the 1930s, burgoo was made from wild meat such as rabbit, squirrel, venison, or opossum. It is typically made in a large pot and stirred with a canoe paddle. It is now made with mutton, chicken, or pork at festivals or large gatherings. It is traditionally served with cornbread.

Ladies' Home Journal

Ladies' Home Journal was a "woman's" magazine first published in 1883 and the first American magazine to reach one million subscribers. It was known as one of the "seven sisters" referring to the Pleiades. Its competitors were *Better Homes and*

Gardens, Family Circle, Good Housekeeping, McCall's, Redbook, and Woman's Day. Due to changing values and lifestyles for women, LHJ could no longer compete and folded in 2016. I would say it had a good run though.

Lady Emma Hamilton (1765-1815)

Lady Hamilton was an English model and courtesan. She was the favorite model of artist George Romney. Emma Hamilton is best known for her love affair with Lord Horatio Nelson, savior of Great Britain from Napoleon Bona-parte. Because they weren't married, Nelson's deathbed instructions for Emma's financial care were ignored and she died destitute at the age of forty-nine.

Lexington, Kentucky Newspapers

Prior to computers and TV, everyone received their news via daily newspapers. Lexington had a morning newspaper and an evening newspaper—the Lexington Herald and the Lexington Leader. When news began to be broadcast on TV, newspaper readership eroded. Lexington could not support two newspapers, so they combined in 1983 to form the Lexington Herald Leader. In

2004, the Herald Leader apologized on behalf of their predecessors for not covering the Civil Rights movement in the Bluegrass. They published a series of articles on the local Civil Rights movement with pictures both papers had documented, but not published in the 1960s. Since 1983, the Herald Leader has won three Pulitzer Awards and been nominated for six more Pulitzers before 2006, surpassing all other midsized newspapers at that time.

Longworth Family

A distinguished family from Cincinnati, Ohio, who made their money from wine. Nicholas Longworth I is remembered as the father of American wine making. Patrons of the arts, they donated land for parks and the Cincinnati Art Museum. Maria Longworth created the Rookwood Pottery Co. Nicholas Longworth III became Speaker of the House and married Alice Roosevelt. His campaigning for William Howard Taft on the Republican ticket for president, while Theodore Roosevelt also ran for president, caused an irreparable rift in their marriage.

Mint Julep

A bourbon, sugar, mint, and shaved ice concoction served in a sterling cup. It is associated with the Kentucky Derby and Kentucky. Recipe: 1 oz bourbon, 1 tsp of granulated sugar, and water. Pour into a silver cup with fresh mint leaves over shaved ice.

Mona von Bismark (1897-1983)

Mona von Bismark was born in Louisville, Kentucky and raised by her grandmother in Lexington, Kentucky. She was an American socialite and fashion icon who was the first Amerian to be named "The Best Dressed Woman in the World." She married five times, including Harrison Williams and Edward von Bismarck-Schonhausen, some of the richest men in the world. My character, Lady Elsmere, aka June Webster, from the Josiah Reynolds Mysteries is based on Mona von Bismark.

New Deal

New Deal was a term taken from Franklin D. Roosevelt's acceptance speech for the presidential Democratic nomination on July 2nd, 1932. He was voted into the US presidency in November after the public reacted negatively to the ineffectiveness of President Herbert Hoover in regards to the Great Depression, which he said would only last a few weeks in 1929. By 1932, the country was dissatisfied with Hoover's policies, and Americans swept the Democratic Party into office with the promise of a "new deal" for the "forgotten man."

New Deal policies were enacted within the first three months of Roosevelt's presidency, which became known as the "Hundred Days." Agencies such as the Works Progress Administration (WPA) and the Civilian Conservation Corps (CCC) were established to provide temporary employment. The WPA provided 8.5 million jobs, produced 650,000 miles of roads, built 125,000 public buildings, 75,000 bridges, and 8,000 parks. Also included in the national bills were the Federal Art Project, Federal Writers' Project, and the Federal Theatre Project to document the Great Depression.

Nineteenth Amendment (Amendment XIX) to the US Constitution

The 19th Amendment to the United States Constitution prohibits the states and the federal government from denying the right to vote to citizens of the United States on the basis of sex. It needed thirty-six states to pass the amendment, and Tennessee was the last state of the thirty-six to do so with only one vote passing it. Harry Burn, who was anti-suffrage for women, received a note from his mother, Phoebe Ensminger Burn, stating, "Hurrah, and vote for suffrage," and implored him to be a "good son." Harry did what his mother wanted and cast the last vote for suffrage breaking the tie. The amendment was adopted in 1920 but was challenged by Leser v Garnett and Fairchild v Hughes. Some states refused to vote on the amendment while other states, mostly in the South, rejected it. States would reverse their rejection of the amendment in favor of it as late as 1984. One vote *can* make all the difference. Thank you, Mrs. Burn, for sending that note to your son.

Noblesse oblige

Noblesse oblige is the responsibility of those living in privilege to act with generosity toward those less fortunate. It is associated with people of high rank or birth.

Pinkerton National Detective Agency

The Pinkertons is a private security firm created by Allan Pinkerton in the 1850s. The agency performed services ranging from security guarding to private military work. At the height of their power, they were hired by wealthy businessmen to infiltrate unions and intimidate workers. During the Homestead Strike of 1892, the Pinkertons confronted striking steel workers, causing the death of three Pinkertons and nine workers. The Pinkerton Agency is now a division of a Swedish company—Securitas AB.

Primogeniture

Primogeniture is an exclusive right of inheritance belonging to the eldest son. Male primogeniture was abolished for the British monarchy in 2011 under a reform by the coalition government, allowing first-born daughters to assume the throne. At the time, peers prevented the reform from applying to them.

Prostitution

Prostitution in Lexington began in 1790 and spurred centuries of unethical and illegal behavior. Lexington citizens complained about the red-light district promoting venereal disease, rowdy behavior, property destruction, and gangs of young men roaming the streets. In 1913, a grand jury indicted the owners of various bawdy houses along "Babylon Block." Among many others, Belle Brezing was indicted for running a bawdy house and selling liquor without a license. In 1915, a committee was formed to study the problem of prostitution in Lexington. This committee brought in experts from the American Social Hygiene Association. One of the things the ASHA did was to compare Lexington's problem of prostitution to other cities. They discovered that Lexington with a population of 40,000 had approximately the same number of prostitutes as Richmond, Virginia which supported a population of 150,000.

Rotary Club

Rotary Club is a non-religious and non-political organization comprised of business and professional people who encourage ethical standards and good works. Women were allowed to join in 1987, and the clubs continue to exist all over the world.

Shotgun Houses

A shotgun house is a narrow home usually twelve feet wide with rooms comprised of a living room, bedroom, and kitchen facing one long hallway with doors at the front and back. It was the most popular style of house from 1861 to the 1920s. Bathrooms were added later. It was called this because one could shoot a gun from the front of the house to the back without hitting a wall.

Stenography

The art of writing in shorthand strives to take dictation as fast as a person is speaking. Most secretaries knew Gregg shorthand in the 1930s, which was a system of elliptical symbols substituted for words. John Robert Gregg invented this shorthand of writing in 1888. Another system of shorthand is the stenotype machine which has 22 keys to type numbers, phrases, words, and sounds by creating a form of phonetic transcription.

Theodore Roosevelt (1858-1919)

He was the 26th president (1901-1909) of the United States. He was known for saying "Walk softly and carry a big stick" which was based on an African proverb—"Walk softly and carry a big stick. You'll go far." This was the basis of Roosevelt's foreign policy to appear benign, but to use force if necessary when national interests were threatened. He is known as a conservationist and created the United States Forest Service, thereby, establishing 150 national forests, 51 federal bird reserves, 4 national game preserves, and 5 national parks. During his presidency, Roosevelt protected 230 million acres of public land. In 1916, President Woodrow Wilson would continue Roosevelt's work by creating the National Park Service. As for his daughter, Alice Roosevelt Longworth, Roosevelt said, "I can be President of the United States or I can control Alice. I cannot possibly do both."

William Donovan (1883-1959)

Donovan was an American soldier, lawyer, and intelligence officer. Donovan is the only veteran to receive all four of the United States highest awards—the Medal of Honor, the Distinguished Service Cross, the Distinguished Service Medal, and the National Security Medal plus the Silver Star and the Purple Heart. He is best known for serving as the head of the Office of Strategic

Services (OSS) during WWII. Another famous alumnus of the OSS was French gourmet chef, Julia Child. The OSS evolved to become the Central Intelligence Agency (CIA) after 1945. Donovan was recruited by President Roosevelt in 1934 to "casually" collect information against Nazis living in the U.S. as the States did not have a formal protocol since spying was frowned upon. Secretary of State Henry L. Stimson, under President Hoover, wrote in his memoirs, "Gentlemen do not read each other's mail," and pulled funding for intelligence gathering. Roosevelt knew that Donovan was a loud critic of such action and felt the U.S. needed a formal intelligence department like the United Kingdom's MI6. As soon as the U.S. was attacked in 1941, Roosevelt demanded that he be granted money for such a department with Donovan heading it. Thus began the OSS. Years later, Donovan died after developing dementia, taking all his secrets with him to the grave. A statue of Donovan stands in the CIA Headquarters lobby. Keep this man in mind. He will pop up in other Mona Moon books.

Venereal Disease
Another name for STDs—sexually transmitted diseases.

Wilkie Collins (1824-1889)
Collins was an English novelist who is credited with writing the first modern English detective novel. Famous for *The Woman In White* 1859 and *The Moonstone* 1868.

Women's Working Rights
From the liberal views of the 1920s, the 1930s became more conservative. It was difficult for women to obtain work, especially in locales where women were thought to belong in the home. Women, who worked outside the home, were criticized for taking jobs away from men and were pressured to quit. Women were even blamed for the Great Depression with some claiming that if women would give up their jobs, unemployment would be eliminated. Of course, these detractors didn't acknowledge the alarming number of single parent households headed by women because their male partners had deserted them. This was called a "poor man's divorce." It was estimated that two million men became

traveling hobos. Yes, women became hobos as well, but not as often as men.

Women were not allowed credit/loans on their own without a male co-signer. In *Dolores Claiborne,* Stephen King does a wonderful job illustrating how a bank allowed a man to steal his wife's money after years of her working and saving.

Working Girls

1930s slang synonymous with prostitutes.

Books By Abigail Keam

Josiah Reynolds Mysteries

Mona Moon Mysteries

About The Author

Abigail Keam is an award-winning and Amazon best-selling author. She is a beekeeper, loves chocolate, and lives on a cliff overlooking the Kentucky River. Besides the *1930s Mona Moon Mysteries*, she writes the award-winning *Josiah Reynolds Mysteries*, *The Princess Maura Tales* (fantasy) and the *Last Chance For Love Series* (sweet romance).

Don't forget to leave a review! Tell your friends about Mona.

Thank you again, gentle reader, for your reviews and your word of mouth, which are so important for any book. I hope to meet you again between the pages.

www.ingramcontent.com/pod-product-compliance
Lightning Source LLC
Chambersburg PA
CBHW060922190726
48286CB00002B/597